1/19

UNCONVENTIONAL WARFARE

CHRIS LYNCH

SPECIAL FORCES

UNCONVENTIONAL WARFARE

BOOK 1

3 1379 02836 0221

SCHOLASTIC PRESS ★ NEW YORK

Library of Congress Cataloging-in-Publication Data available.

ISBN 978-0-545-86162-5

10 9 8 7 6 5 4 3 2 1   18 19 20 21 22

First edition, December 2018

Printed in the U.S.A. 23
Book design by Christopher Stengel

CHAPTER ONE

True Tough

I was beating the tar out of my brother Edgar. And because Edgar was born with an abnormal amount of tar in him, beating it out was nearly a full-time, full-on job.

I had him by the neck, by the throat, pressed deep into the upholstery of Dad's big wingback reading chair. There was no question I was winning this fight, just as there was never any question of who was winning our frequent, spirited, intense confrontations. That would be me.

No question except, I suppose, in the mind of Edgar. That was one place I would never want to go, personally, even to find out how he thought he'd wiggle out of my grip. But his face was helpful enough. Turning plum purple, and with his strength draining so quickly I could feel it running down my arms and torso and onto the floor, he still managed to lay that vile and infuriating toothy leer on me.

Which, naturally, drove me berserk. As it was intended to.

I threw my whole life-force into the effort of strangling my brother and breaking his neck and putting him personally into his final resting place directly beneath our house. The chair flew backward, and Edgar flew backward, and I flew forward without ever losing my grip. The thunder-crash as we hit the floor was somehow not quite enough, so I went onward and jackhammered Edgar's head against the hardwood floor. I just wanted to get that victory expression off his face because, in all fairness, it was all wrong in this instance.

"Stop it! Stop, Danny, stop!" My other brother, Kent, screamed as he slammed into me from the side, toppling me but failing to break my grip.

"Idiot, I'm doing this for you!" I screamed back.

"Well you can stop doing it for me!"

"No, I can't. I can't stop," I said, pinning Edgar to the floor with my right hand and shoving Kent's face away with my left.

A crack of knuckles to the tip of my chin sent my head snapping back. Edgar seized his moment.

"One hand?" Edgar yelled as he rolled me backward and jumped on me. "You think you can hold me down with *one* hand, Danny?"

He wasn't appalled by many things, my brother, but he was rightly appalled at that. Because while I always beat him, always, I didn't always beat him easily or by much. It was a brothers thing, where you know one another so well, without even knowing *what* you know, that you can turn a sure mismatch into a real contest. If you have the guts for it.

My brothers had the guts for it.

Even Kent, who looked like he wouldn't give your average badminton player much trouble, could scrap like a wild dog when he had to. So we had our pecking order in our house. Edgar whomped on Kent, and then I whomped on Edgar for whomping on Kent. I felt like it was my job and my duty, no matter how hard or how fun that job was. And no matter whether Kent appreciated me for it or not.

With my back flat on the floor and Edgar on my chest, I balled my left fist, zeroed in on his puggy nose . . . and then Kent lunged. He grabbed my arm before I could let fly.

"No, Danny, stop!" Kent squawked, though I could barely hear him over Edgar's howl of delight. He could neither believe his luck nor contain his joy. Edgar thanked Kent by popping me a sharp, snapping left jab, right off of my forehead.

"Kent!" I bellowed. I wasn't even much bothered with Edgar anymore, since he was only doing exactly what he should have done in that situation. I'd have been angry if he *didn't* punch me with a sweet opportunity like that.

In one super heave, I blasted Edgar right off of me, sending him crashing into the base of the front door. Then, I went for Kent.

"You idiot," I barked as I gave him a hard backhand across his cheek. "You don't break up a fight by holding one guy's arm down so the other guy can pound him! How do you not know that? Have you been paying attention at all?" He was paying attention now as I bapped him across the face. Back and forth and back and forth with my right hand, while I held him still with my left.

"I didn't want you to kill my brother," he protested.

"You didn't want . . . *I'm* your brother! And I was flat on my back!"

"Yeah, Kent," Edgar said, enjoying his seat on the floor. "Danny was *losing*."

"I was *never* losing," I shouted, turning toward Edgar just as the front door opened and cracked him right in the back.

"Ha!" I roared, still cuffing Kent casually into submission.

Then I saw it was Dad coming through the door.

I immediately felt bad, but there was nothing I could do about it now. I ceased all movement, though, releasing my grip on Kent.

"Why?" Dad wailed, in that way of his. In just the way I knew he would. He had a low note he would hit at times, when we did stuff that wounded and saddened him. That note wounded and saddened me, too. Then he balled his fists up the best he could, and hit it again. "Why, Daniel? Why can't you just leave them be?" He looked down, as if yelling at the rug. His hands trembled with the intensity of his anguish. The left fist he threatened the floor with looked like a normal fist. But the right one, the withered one, shook worse.

I couldn't look his disappointment straight on. So I had to do the other thing, the crappy, unfunny, unfair thing.

"I think it's their hair, Pop."

He looked up now, with his fist and his withered hand held unsteady in front of him.

"You think it's what?"

"Oh, not this again, Danny," Edgar barked.

"Not again. Not now," Kent moaned.

They had offensive, antagonistic hair, both of them. Edgar's was bunchy and big, like a snow cone of hair. Kent's was straight and wispy and almost girly long. And it was orange. They both had bright orange punch-me hair. Mine was normal human brown, with a normal side part.

"Half the guys in school have lined up to fight these two because of their hair. How am I supposed to resist when I have to look at it round the clock?"

For a second, I convinced myself I was making a pretty good case. But then something happened that I never saw coming. Something I could not possibly have seen coming because it had never happened before. Something that was too unreal to be real and so I didn't believe it was possible, even as I watched it rolling straight toward me.

My dad, my sweet-natured, physically-unfit-for-service-in-two-wars-even-though-he-tried-to-sign-up-for-both father, threw himself forward in an effort to attack me.

"They . . . are . . . not . . . getting . . . in . . . fights . . . because . . . of . . . their . . . *hair*!" Dad wheezed as he flailed awkwardly, clapping me on the chest and shoulders as I stared in complete shock. My brothers jumped in to restrain him. "They are getting in fights, Daniel, because *you* are training them to be chippy, combative ruffians! You mold them in your own image, so they'll fight with anything that moves, for no apparent reason!"

I had never seen him so upset. I had never *felt*, inside myself, so upset. Things did not upset me. That was part of my package, part of how this machine worked. But this vision here: My poor old man, enfeebled by polio, then again by post-polio—because life is loaded with great punch lines—who never did anybody any harm ever, was trying with everything he had to harm me. And everything he had barely amounted to anything. My poor dad couldn't even throw me off balance. Not physically, at least.

But it paralyzed me all the same. My arms hung at my sides as he tried and tried to get at me. Dad's strength rapidly ran down, and both Edgar and Kent tried to assure him in low voices that everything was all right, but he wasn't assured in any way. I wanted to tell him I was sorry. But nothing came out of me. When I couldn't get it out in time, Dad finally started crying. Giving up. He just let my brothers hold him, weeping away.

I was not going to cry, no, it just wasn't going to happen because that was not how this machine worked.

But all the strength that had to be diverted to holding back my tears made it even more impossible to tell Dad I was sorry and that I would do better.

He deserved to hear that at least. But no. The machine was in high gear.

He could cry. How come I couldn't?

Finally, I snapped out of my stupor. I blew past all three of them and bolted out the front door.

"Why do you have to do these things?" he wailed, just before I had time to slam the door between me and his words.

Not that I'd have had an answer for him. I didn't know why I had to do those things. I just had to, was all.

Anyway, Edgar and Kent were lucky to have me around, to be honest. It was me making those two sad-sack brothers of mine into hard nuts who could handle anything that came their way. That's what I figured. No way could Dad have ever taught them the stuff I taught them.

Although there was one big thing I could never teach them. That was how to be as tough as the toughest guy I ever knew.

Dad.

"Daniel!"

Oh, no, please.

I was quickstep-walking away from the house and that scene, faster than most people could run. I didn't lose any pace as I looked back over my shoulder to verify what I already knew.

"Go home, Dad!" I yelled.

That was pointless, of course. Once I looked back, he had me hooked, and he knew it.

I stopped fast-walking, started backward-walking as I watched the old man put every which kind of energy into going not very fast at all. I stopped backward-walking and came to a stop. Dad wore a brace on his left leg that turned every other stride into a small pole-vaulting action. Made no difference to him as he huffed and hobbled down that sidewalk to get to me. His good left arm pumped the way anybody's arm would when running, only it pumped at about a three-to-one rate compared to his right one.

To look at his strained face, his frantic body language, you would find no sign that he didn't believe he'd eventually catch me. Even when I started walking toward him to make the trip just marginally shorter, he didn't let up one tiny bit on the gas.

He practically fell into my arms with exhaustion when we finally came together. I held on to him as he struggled to catch his breath. And he held on to me as best he could.

We hung on like that for a few minutes. Which was good. Without saying anything. Which was even better.

CHAPTER TWO

Triumph

If this bike didn't take your breath away then either you never had any breath to begin with, or you didn't deserve the breath you had.

It was the exact, approximate model that Steve McQueen rode in *The Great Escape*. You just knew that every joker in every theater in every country in the world, with the possible exception of Germany—and even that possibility was beyond distant—was watching Steve McQueen in that movie with their jaws planted flat on the sticky, disgusting cinema floor.

Most folks thought, by the way, that it was a BMW bike Mr. Steve was riding, since BMWs were the chosen bikes of the Nazis. And while being a Nazi bike would have been no fault of the machine's, Steve McQueen was not riding a BMW in those thrilling scenes. The bike that was made to look like a World War II German BMW was, in fact, a Triumph.

That event in history was a Triumph, just as the machine was a Triumph. And at this very moment, cruising down the highway at I-don't-know-how-many miles per hour on a real Steve McQueen replica, I also felt very much like a Triumph.

I had never felt anything in my life like the sensation of tearing down the midnight road at the controls of this magnificent man-made force of nature. And I knew, pretty much instantly, that I would spend the whole rest of my life in pursuit of exactly this thing I had in my power right now.

Who wouldn't?

The only problem, I suppose, was that it wasn't my motorcycle. Yeah, that was probably a large part of the problem, but there was a lot more to it than that.

"Yeah, yeah, yeah," Mr. Macias said in that voice of his that could have sounded tired, but seemed to me more like something withheld. A voice restraining itself. "Sure, there was a lot more to it than that. There's *always* a lot more to it than that."

He was leading me down the hall and out of the police station at about one o'clock on a Monday morning, which rightly still belonged to Sunday night. Mr. Macias was, among other things, my wrestling coach and practically my own personal guidance counselor. Months ago, he'd told me I could call him in the very likely event I found myself in trouble. Those were his very words, and *this* was that very trouble.

"But maybe this particular instance," I continued, "is the accumulation of a whole bunch of other *more-to-its*. Maybe you should just *listen* to me if you really want to hear my side of the story!"

Mr. Macias had pushed through the two hefty glass doors of the police station and marched right down its four granite steps to the sidewalk. He stood, turned crisply on his heel, and addressed me directly.

"Daniel *Manion*," he growled. "Do you honestly mean to question my commitment to you, after you've just woken me from the deep depths of sleep? After I came basically *running* down to the station to make sure you were being treated fairly, do you truly believe I might still be thinking, 'Surely, the kid couldn't possibly have anything interesting to say for himself'?"

I took a deep breath. To compose.

He spoke lower and slower now, which might have appeared to be a positive sign. I knew it was no such thing. "You actually need time to think about your answer, Danny?"

"Yes, sir, Mr. Macias . . . I mean, no, no, not at all.

I was just trying to get the right form of words to match the form of your question. So I wouldn't get it wrong by accident. Like if somebody asks 'Have you ever not killed a man in self-defense?' And you answer—"

He struck like a sidewinder, his strong hand seizing me by the shirt collar and guiding me down the street in the direction of home. "No," he said sharply.

"No?" I chirped my confusion.

"No, Danny. No. No was your right answer, because no, you would not ever question my commitment to you."

"No," I said, and he released his grip so we could walk along in a more normal side-by-sidewinder fashion. "No, sir, Mr. Macias, I never would question that."

And I never, ever would. It really was simply about the form of the words. Because he was equally as committed to being precise and correct in the use of language as he was to being precise and correct about everything else.

After a generous few silent strides, walking briskly in lockstep, Mr. Macias wasn't going to wait any longer. "So?" he asked.

"So?" I asked.

"So, Daniel, what is the more? 'More to it than that,' is what you told me. At the very least, I think I deserve to hear your explanation for why an intelligent and not entirely demented young man would steal and crash a motorcycle, not to mention what possessed you to be out on the street cruising around like a mischief-seeking missile at such a late hour on a *school* night. I'd say I deserve to hear that, Mr. Manion, wouldn't you?"

"I would, sir. I definitely would. But now, since you said all that there, I'm feeling like I'm not going to have quite enough *more to it* to cover the situation."

This was where he could have gotten mean. This was where he would probably be *justified* in getting mean, for all the stupidity I was spraying over us both. It wasn't like I was trying to be stupid. There was nothing that'd fill me with more dread than the possibility of pushing Mr. Roland Macias to anger. Everyone at school felt exactly that way, too.

He was a force, Mr. Macias was. A power, a mystery, and a legend. Every last student in the whole school would agree that we had one genuine legend on our staff, though no one could really say *why* we believed it. Nobody really knew anything about the guy, his life outside of school, or his history, beyond the rough out-line they gave us when he showed up at the beginning of the year. Recently retired military man, Rhodes scholar, two-time NCAA wrestling champion, and, possibly, Batman.

He made no effort, as far as I could tell, to suggest anything unusual lurked behind his oversize reading glasses. But that just made the Batman theory all the more plausible.

Maybe his aura was due to the stare. Come to think of it, yeah, it had to be the stare. I'd have wagered real money that he was capable of starting fires with that stare if he felt like it.

He was doing it to me right now, eyeing me intently while still pounding the pavement straight ahead.

"Okay, for starters, Mr. Macias, I didn't *steal* that motorcycle. See, I know whose bike it is, and so that part of it is cool."

"That's swell, Dan. That sorts everything out. But you know who else knows whose bike it is? The *owner* of the bike. Ricky Siber. And the police know who the real owner of the bike is, too, because they were told when Ricky Siber was good enough to phone them up and tell them that you stole his motorcycle."

"A misunderstanding, Mr. Macias. I'll talk to Ricky myself tomorrow and everything will be just—"

"Oh, right, you'll talk to him tomorrow? Smooth everything over?"

"Yeah, something like that."

"Uh-huh. Now tell me, was it that smooth talking of yours that landed you and Mr. Siber in the jug for a week of detention after your fight?"

Oh. People and their memories sometimes.

"Mr. Macias, come on, you know how it is. Even the best of friends can get in a little scrap or two over time."

"I do know how it is, and I also know that *five* fights do not constitute a scrap or two."

This was the kind of thing that could spook you about the man. I didn't have any idea he paid serious attention to the one or two fights I might have had in the school-yard, but he sure did.

And as for the three other times, I'd taken fathead Siber all the way down to the old quarry—a mile and a half from school property—in order to bounce his smug face off of some granite boulders in peace and seclusion. There should have been no way Mr. Macias could know about those.

He took the wind out of me there. When I couldn't get anything useful to come out of my slack open mouth, he took charge of the conversation.

"Five fights with one guy? What are you hoping to achieve?"

"Siber has a big mouth."

"And you have a short temper."

"Maybe. But he still needed to be taught some lessons. So I did it. Took him to *school*, five times out of five."

"Four times out of five."

"*What?*" I should have been able to keep my composure there, to deny him the satisfaction. But he had me. Siber had done all right in his last fight. He'd wriggled out of his lesson, which is why new teaching methods had been required.

"Come on, Manion. Who do you think you're dealing with here?"

I absolutely did not know. I knew Mr. M taught Spanish and History, was a guidance counselor and wrestling coach. He had a beard. Sort of shaggy hair, too, and he wasn't wildly fussed about fashionable attire. He sort of looked like Jesus with muscles, and gave off an air that he might be more willing to use them than Jesus probably would.

I'd once caught a glimpse of him staring down an unruly parent—some goon father of a goon sophomore who'd taken issue with his kid's suspension. Mr. Macias didn't know I was looking. He had this focus to him, like he was a hunter with an elk or a leopard in his sights and was going to bring it down in one sudden shot.

Both Goon and Goon Jr. had walked away that day, grumbling but accepting. The suspension stood.

"I know who I'm dealing with, sir," I said. Respectful, but with the proper bluster.

"No, not really you don't."

Didn't see that one coming.

"Okay, fair enough, I don't. I'd like to, though."

"Maybe at some point you will. Probably not, but maybe. And most definitely not as long as you keep going around behaving like an idiot."

For the first time, he got my back up. I couldn't just let that go.

"I'm not an idiot, sir. I'm not."

"Didn't say you were, because you most certainly aren't. Said you were *behaving* like one. Which is that much worse, because you are *capable* of a whole lot better than you've been showing."

I got a little flush of embarrassment at that. A flush

of embarrassed pride, because a guy didn't hear a thing like that too often. And he certainly didn't hear it from the likes of Mr. Macias, who disapproved of tossing bouquets at students for getting the test scores and match victories they should have expected to get all along.

Just so things didn't get at all mushy between us, what came out of me was this: "If I haven't been showing it, how would you know what I was capable of?"

Sometimes embarrassment can make you say some unwise wise-guy things.

Mr. Macias simply stayed quiet. Walked a bit faster, but other than that there was no sign of irritation, distraction, contemplation—or anything else that would explain why he needed time to respond.

"Mr. Macias?" I tried, picking up my pace to match his.

"I'm not quite sure how to handle it with your dad."

"Dad? He'll be fine. One way or another, he's always fine. He won't give me too much trouble over this, so really, there's no reason to worry about him. I'll handle him."

If my embarrassed pride remark made him vaguely displeased, this one removed any vagueness.

Mr. Macias sped up and then pulled in front of me,

like one car cutting off another in traffic. *Unlike* a car in traffic, however, he pivoted and got his nose and eyes aligned really close up with mine.

"There is every reason to worry about him. He is your *dad*. Do you understand?"

"I understand. Of course I understand. I see the guy every morning and every evening. He just keeps coming back, is all. Can't imagine why anyone would submit to so much time with me and my two stenchy mongrel brothers, unless he was genetically obligated to do so."

"So you think I'm out here in the middle of the night, providing cover for your silly butt—when your silly butt deserves all the kicking it could get—simply because I want to spare you embarrassment?"

I paused, trying to work all that out. I should not have paused.

"Your father, *the* Mr. Manion, deserves a lot better than to be troubled with any more of your antics than necessary."

While I couldn't quite put my finger on it, I had the strong sense that there were more than a couple of little digs at me in there. And frankly, after listening to cops call me sixteen different kinds of scum hoodlum for an hour, I wasn't in the mood to listen to any more of it.

"How do you know that, Mr. Macias, huh? How do you know what he deserves? Maybe I'm just exactly what he deserves."

"How do I know he deserves better? Because everyone's father deserves better. Better than *this*, that's for sure."

He had a step on me, so when he jerked his thumb in my direction at the word *this*, it was right on target, mid-chest. Felt like I took an elbow more than a thumb; it was sharp and it scored. I hated that, being thumbed at. Just hated it. I wanted to thump him one right in the kidney.

"Don't even think about it," he said, without a sideways glance at me.

I hated *that* even more. Boy, did I hate it when he came over all-seeing, all-knowing, like some Navajo shaman or an Indian mystic or something. Blood-boiling stuff, and he knew it. He probably *thought* I was going to take a nutty over it. Which was why a nutty was exactly what I would not be taking. Because I'd rather hold it inside and risk dying from my own toxic internal combustion than allow him the Triple Crown of knowitallability.

"You have to breathe eventually, Danny," he said with the easy humor of a guy who is, in fact, always right.

It came bursting out like a particularly angry belch

I'd been holding in. "You're not always right, y'know, Mr. Macias. You don't know everything."

And I'm sure he also knew that I needed this, needed to be provoked into blowing off steam, because he just turned around and kept walking. He quickened his pace a little and possibly even chuckled as I continued snarling in his direction.

"Because you can't know everything. Nobody can. Nobody does. Nobody knows everything there is to know about anything, never mind knowing everything about everything. Nobody knows me, I'll tell you that right now. Nobody knows me and nobody's gonna, either, because that's the way I like it. And you don't know my life or my house or the people who live inside it or what goes on in there. You don't know. Maybe you know about where *you* came from, what maybe your own father did or didn't do that's got you so worked up on the whole sacred father deal, but that's you, not me. Maybe . . ." I let myself fade out there for a few seconds. Not because I was finished with my mission yet, but because I'd caught the scent of a joke that was going to aid my cause nicely. "For all you know, my father might be completely *lame*." I chuckled there, fake and mean, whinnied loudly like a deranged horse. Even though *any* kind of laugh felt suddenly, deeply unfunny.

And yet I persisted, of course I did. To this day I have no idea why. "Maybe I'm the ratman I apparently am as a direct result of having the lamest lame spaz of a father anybody ever had." I even did the little hand spasm thing my dad did, just in case I hadn't already qualified as the worst rotten-apple son who ever lived. "Ever think of that, Mr. Macias?"

He had never thought of that. And he surely wasn't thinking it now as he wheeled on me with a fury I had never known. He practically left his feet in the effort of giving my snotty mug the full brunt of his furious stare.

Nobody had ever looked at me like that.

"I have watched that father of yours drag himself to every meet, every match you or your brothers ever wrestled. I saw him shovel his car out of the school lot, one-handed, while all three able-bodied Manion boys were too dazzled by a sudden snowstorm to do anything more useful than pelt one another with snowballs in the face. I heard him holler and heard him cheer in some of those godforsaken icebox gyms halfway across the state, until it was obvious that the effort was taking the very breath out of him. Then he'd take a break and be back at it five minutes later. I saw the effort that man put into supporting *you* unstintingly. Even, on occasion, when attitudinal unwellness meant that the effort his son brought that day was not entirely worthy of that support."

"Listen, Mr. M, I—"

"No. You listen. Your father deserves your respect. Doing all that father business is hard enough, and a lot of guys don't have the guts to stick around to see it through the way he has. And that's guys with two good arms, legs, and lungs. And a mother, by the way, probably carrying eighty percent of the workload at home."

I had by then gone from hanging my head to embedding my chin a good four inches deep into my collarbone. I was on the verge of burrowing through my own core, to retreat out through the back of myself, when some words managed their way out of me.

"I know. I'm sorry, and I know. Don't know why I said that at all."

"Well, I do," he growled. Mr. Macias got up close to my face. I had the clear impression that this was one of those gentlemen you never, ever wanted to push beyond their limit. "But that's a conversation for another day. The conversation for *this* day is, I don't care even a little bit what drove you to it. You ever speak about your old man in those terms again and the thing that's gotten into you is going to be *me*." He jabbed my chest sharply enough to leave a puncture hole. "Understood?"

I took an extra silent beat to clarify for both of us how much I understood, even though I needed no such beat.

"I never understood a thing more comprehensively in my whole life, Mr. Macias, sir."

CHAPTER THREE

Judgment

Mr. Macias sat next to me as I waited for the judge to enter the room.

We hadn't *exactly* kept the fact that I was headed to court from Dad, but Mr. M had told him that it wouldn't be a big enough deal that my father needed to miss any work over it. After all, how many jobs were out there for typesetters in printing houses? Despite his handicap, Dad was a calligraphy whiz. He ran a small art department, where he could still hand-letter a special order now and then. There were many different ways in which my dad was one of a kind.

"You're sure you're okay?" Mr. Macias asked, as the judge appeared and we all rose.

"Of course I'm okay," I said. I was always okay. "Why wouldn't I be?"

We sat back down and the judge called up the case of some clueless dope who'd set his girlfriend's house on fire. A crime of passion, his lawyer called it.

"A crime of mental defectiveness," I muttered.

"Reminds me of you," Mr. M said. "Doesn't he remind you of you? Around the eyes a bit, and the frontal lobe area?"

"That is *not* me," I hissed.

"Okay," he said. And we both went quiet.

Stayed quiet, too, through the procession of people my father would call ne'er-do-wells. Guys who were in court for doing incredibly stupid things.

"You okay *now*?" Mr Macias asked again, when there were only a couple of cases left to hear.

"I'm *fine*," I said. "I told you I'm always okay, so why do you keep asking?"

"Because this isn't always, and you are not going to be okay."

"What—?"

"The Court calls Daniel Manion."

The Court called, and I had no choice but to answer.

The weary gray man with the gavel, Judge Salisbury, had no interest in wasting time on the likes of me.

"You've been here before, I see," the judge said.

"Yes, sir," I answered.

"In the past three years you've commandeered a motorbike, a boat . . . and a small twin-engine aircraft that did not belong to you."

"Well, actually—" I said . . . before Mr. Macias put a death grip on my arm.

"True, your honor." My court-appointed representative spoke when I could not.

"Did you actually try to jump across the old Haussler quarry?" the judge asked.

"When the wind is behind me, it's not a problem," I answered honestly.

He seemed to be chuckling as he dropped his head, ran his hand through his very judge-like gray hair, and studied my history. Then he looked up. "And you managed to fly that plane when you were thirteen years old?"

"More or less," I said, feeling the pride-smile open up across my face. "It was more *less* than *more*, I guess, but I did get up to where I was no longer stuck to planet Earth. So, that counts, I figure."

He nodded, looked down again, finger-combed his hair again. Possibly chuckled again. He was a good guy, I could tell, and he understood. I relaxed a little.

"You have a remarkable range of skills, Mr. Manion," he said.

I was just about to thank him when I heard Mr. Macias say, "Uh-oh."

"Your grades are excellent. You are a fine athlete. You're obviously fearless . . ."

Again, I was just about to say either *thank you* or *aw, shucks*, but Mr. M trumped me with another "Uh-oh."

"Wha-aat?" I whispered, before Judge Salisbury clarified things.

"But as impressive as all that may be, there are rules, son. There are rules that apply to living in this free society, and there are penalties that come with consistently flouting those rules. So, while I am left with very few options in dealing with a repeat offender, I am now going to be magnanimous in offering *you* a choice between two. You can either go to the juvenile offenders institution, or enlist in the institution that made a man out of me— the United States Marines. Because frankly, at this point, your country needs you, but I do not."

I was rigid with shock. None of this was what I had expected.

Mr. Macias squeezed my arm in a more comforting way. I felt instantly better. He would sort this out. He gestured to the judge, who then waved him up to discuss things in private. I knew things would be okay. They talked for maybe half a minute. The judged frowned fiercely, but nodded eventually, and Mr. M came back to stand by my side.

"After considering the advice of a friend of the Court . . ." Judge Salisbury announced, and I could taste freedom already, "I have reconsidered."

"Thank you," I said to Mr. Macias.

"You're welcome," he said.

"Instead of the Marines, you will be permitted to enlist in . . . the United States Army."

I whipped my head around to face Mr. Macias.

I was not sure if I had ever seen him smile before. But I sure was seeing it now.

My father once said I wasn't tough enough.

Said I wasn't tough enough, wasn't smart enough, brave enough, strong enough, motivated enough, athletic enough, or tall enough.

That's what he said when I told him I was trying out for the basketball team. It wasn't exactly *Go get 'em, kid*, but it was better than I had expected. At least he drove me there.

When I failed to make the final cut for the team, he was there for me. There in the parking lot to pick me up in the smoky Studebaker that had both the paint color and the exhaust fumes of a tire fire. On the drive home he gave me the exact same laundry list of my shortcomings.

This might give you the impression that Dad was one of those heartless, back-breaking, sneering, over-critical ogre kind of fathers. If so, then I'd be giving the wrong impression.

He did say all those things, and said them lots of times, so the facts themselves are in order. The impression should be modified, however. Because he didn't voice all that out of some kind of mean-spiritedness.

He said it because he loved me. He loved me so much that he spent every day of my existence anxious for me to be able to take care of myself, to survive whatever this rough ol' life might throw at me. He wanted me to be a man who could beat the world, no matter what game the world was playing.

He wanted me to be the World-beater.

The World-beater that he could never be. He was always apologizing that he was physically unable to be that *for* me, like he thought a father was supposed to be. The polio had seen to that. I hated it so much when he apologized for himself, and I told him so, loudly and often.

That only made him switch to apologizing for something else that wasn't his fault. For not being my mother. For nobody being my mother.

That was just stupid, and I told him so, loudly and often.

I didn't need a mother. Didn't care about not having a mother. Didn't even know what I'd do with one if she showed up. It'd be a waste.

It was Dad and me and Edgar and Kent, and that seemed about right to me. Sure, there were some hilarious jokers in school who liked to compare us to the TV show *My Three Sons*. The program was about a family that was statistically the same as us, but was actually made up of a bunch of stiffs who wore button-down sweaters. Even my dad on his worst days was nowhere near as rigid as the father on *My Three Sons*.

Anyway. When he said I wasn't tough enough, it meant a whole bunch of other things, mostly about his own heart and not my ability to get through all the come-what-mays.

Then there was this. He wanted me out of the house, away from the boys, but he never wanted this.

"Are you going to be okay?" he asked when I told him about my enlistment. "Are you sure you're tough enough for this?" His eyes welled up as he said it.

CHAPTER FOUR

Top of the World

I am riding nearly nine feet off the ground, with five tons of Asian elephant beneath me, crossing the Laotian border into the central highlands of Vietnam. I'm in the middle of a convoy of three massive beasts who could qualify as their own mountain range except for the swaying back and forth, the undulating that threatens to throw us off and into the jungle at any time.

And the crapping. Oh, the crapping, my goodness all that crapping. I'm part of a six-man task force dispatched from a place we're supposedly not allowed to be, to rescue one of our men who's technically not even a member of the American military team. He's a pilot for Bird & Sons, which is a private contract cargo airline that just happens to do a lot of contract cargo work for the Good Guys—who are us. One of their main contracts is to resupply the trailwatch teams who monitor the movement of goods and materials in secret. We watch a long network of connected roads, reaching all the way from North Vietnam, through Laos and Cambodia, and into South Vietnam. The Communists use these trails to resupply their forces.

They aren't supposed to operate in Laos, according to the Geneva Accords of 1962. Apparently the Communists don't care.

Of course, our trailwatch teams aren't supposed to be there, either. Nor are any of our other teams. But what are we supposed to do, just not watch them? They need watching.

So everybody's breaking the rules. And since breaking rules was more or less how I wound up here in the first place . . . I don't have a whole lotta problem with it.

Truth is, there are no rules here. It's glorious. If there are no rules, maybe that makes me the ruler.

Yeah, it probably does.

Trailwatching, though, is how I got to know a bunch of those Bird & Sons guys. And good guys, every last one of them.

So, an extraction mission to save any one of them is a duty and a pleasure.

We are stopped for a break, at the point where there is no more *up* for us to climb and we're about to make the final descent into the enemy camp to take back our boy. The physical nature of riding the elephants is fairly demanding, requiring more frequent stops than, say, a gentle troop-truck journey. Poop-trucks are rougher than troop-trucks. Especially for some of us.

"Lopez," I say as quietly as I can, despite my enthusiasm for the topic, "how much are you loving this elephant stuff?"

"How much am I loving it?" Lopez replies, massaging his own rump with both hands. "Not at all much, is how much, Bug. I hate them. But that's okay, because that is exactly the same way they feel about me, so I'm not gonna feel bad about it."

I'm laughing because I already know this, but I never get tired of hearing it. I never get tired of hearing almost anything my pal Lopez says, because he says everything as if it's the most infuriating thing in the world. Or the funniest. Or the saddest. Or the reddest, ugliest, stupidest . . .

"Stop laughing at me, Bug."

"No. Not possible. Never. Even the elephants are laughing. You're a very funny person."

"They are not laughing. They are not humorous. I am not a very funny person. And neither are you, by the way."

"Wrong on all counts. And someday you'll see. I'm gonna get one of these great beasts for myself soon."

"Your own elephant?"

"Yup."

"And where you figure you're gonna keep it?"

"I don't know. In my hat."

"Well, it'll fit, that's for sure."

"Ha!" I say, smacking him on his prized North Vietnamese Army–issue pith helmet. "Who says you're not funny?"

"I do."

He does, but he shouldn't. Since the day we met at Fort Benning, Georgia, Gust Lopez has been brightening all my days. I call him Gust not only because it's short for Gustavo, but also because he is a mighty wind of righteousness and certainty, no matter what the subject is.

Suddenly, Col. Macias is right in my ear—and when I say he is *right in my ear,* it's not the same way you might say that about other people being right in your ear. I mean I can not only hear the growly hiss of every word, I can not only feel his hot, angry breath tickling my eardrum, I can feel his lips sort of nibbling my ear the way a horse takes a sugar cube.

"Do you two want to shut up, or fall down? Because that's gonna be the choice if you cannot keep your voices quiet, and it's a choice you'll be making for *all* of us when you draw enemy fire and get us all killed."

"I think we'll go with shutting up, Colonel," I whisper.

"Yes, sir," Gust adds. "Shutting up now. Yes, sir."

We mount back up in complete silence, because while getting bisected at the waist by Vietcong AK-47 fire would be unpleasant, it would be patty-cake compared to the horrors that would follow if Col. Macias had to tell us to shut up again.

He doesn't really like to repeat himself.

And he shouldn't have to. We have been trained. We're the most special Special Forces in the world. And we know it.

We can jump out of planes without breaking our legs. We can put a bullet up a man's nose from five hundred yards with the right scope. We know everything you would want to know about the fine art of demolitions. We can raise such thunder with just a handful of C-4 plastic explosive and a few yards of detonation cord, you'd think that God Himself was raging at you. But we *can* be quiet, and we usually are. We'll swim out into a harbor where we know the bad guys are unloading arms, slap a magnetic mine on a hull, and be back on the beach all cozy in time to watch the fireworks.

We know how to sneak up on a sentry so quick and quiet with a KA-BAR knife that his head can look up at his body as it falls down to catch up with it. We were trained as United States Army Rangers, right down to specialist jungle warfare instruction in Panama, which was the most fun I ever had in my life.

And then we were stolen. Just imagine how tough an organization would have to be to steal anything from the Army Rangers.

Technically we weren't stolen, we were *seconded*. I wouldn't have even thought that was a word. Does it mean we can be thirded? Or fourthed?

But hey, I guess if you're a truly *special* Special Operations Group, you can do as you please. Including inventing language.

My elephant, whom I call Dave, might be a secret operative for the enemy, the way he is trying to dump me over one side and then over the other before we ever reach our fallen comrade.

But I'm not going down, no matter how hard he shakes me. I hope he keeps shaking and rocking all the way, because this convoy is the most awesome micro combat force I have ever seen. Especially the way we can move through the jungle, through the night, still managing to keep our secrecy until the moment we come pounding into the enemy compound.

Which we do, right now.

It is almost like a Boy Scout campground that we find, just where our local informants told us we would. There are a half-dozen tent-like structures made of bamboo and leaves, and as we roll up with M16s drawn, we see not a soul because we have caught them completely by surprise.

That is, unless they have all dropped dead from the shock before we even get the chance to shoot them. That's what I'd probably do if I was in their slippers.

But then, here they are.

Each elephant is driven by a Mahout, a local Meo tribesman who knows the animal like a brother. Behind the Mahout on each mount are two commandos leaning out of either side of the basket, guns raised and ready. As the Vietcong fighters roll out of the huts already shooting, the elephants fan out and we open up on every movement in our sights.

It's the smell as much as anything. Six M16s blasting away at once, we make an almighty din. The muzzle flashes just before first light are something brilliant to behold, but the scent of the firepower is intoxicating. I sense it, and off to my right I know Gust does, too. The

Mahouts are right with us, charging ahead after a brief pause, while we slaughter the overpowered VC not just with hundreds of rounds but with enraged mighty beasts who stomp them out like screaming little fires.

An enemy fighter straight in Dave's path takes direct aim at me, and I think for an instant he might have my number. But as we charge ahead I see the very moment where terror overtakes his courage. He screams and the gun drops from his hands involuntarily. I actually pity him while he gamely claws and grabs at the weapon as it scuttles down the front of him. He's trying, bless his soul.

But his soul is his business, and his body is mine.

I pull the trigger while watching him give up on the gun and look straight up into Dave's face. *Pu-pu-pu-pu-pu-pu-pu-pu-pu-puh* . . .

And so on, as I empty all of my ammunition into this brave soldier who would have done the same to me. Who was terrified of my incredible friend Dave, and who was part of a team that was unfortunate enough to be holding our pilot from Bird & Sons.

He hits the ground face-first before Dave reaches him and turns the unholy holey mess of him into pulp.

The sun is coming up orange somewhere ahead of us, beyond the jungle density on the other side of the village.

The elephants are still. The men atop the elephants are still. The men splashed and splayed around the ground in front of us sure are still. For all of the howling mayhem we created just minutes ago, there isn't the slightest echo of that in the air now, unless odors could be considered echoes.

I think they could. Even through all the smoke, I can smell blood and shredded flesh and brains and intestines. Maybe this is influenced by the fact that I am looking at blood and shredded flesh and brains and intestines. Maybe.

When we have waited just long enough, Col. Macias gives the signal and we climb down off our mounts.

"Cool, man," Lopez says low as we step through the bodies on the way to investigate each hut for live human beings.

"Cool, man," I say in return.

There turns out to be only one live human left in the village, as the VC threw every man into their last stand. Remaining, though, is one completely naked Bird & Sons pilot, lashed up and stuffed inside what looks like a bamboo version of a medium-size dog's travel cage.

"Sure am glad to see all yous guys," says the pilot, Donnie Marcotte.

"Same to you," Col. Macias says as Lopez works to get the cage open. "That is, not glad to see *all* of you . . ."

You don't even know, when you go through something like that—when you survive or endure something like that—how much it takes out of you. As I climb up onto Dave for the trip back, I'm trembly and wobbly. Twice I nearly fall to the ground from a good height, before making it safely up. And I can actually feel my basket-mate Lopez shaking as he takes his spot next to me.

"This is exactly what I wanted," he says very quietly as the elephants start swinging and swaying toward Laos again.

"Me too," I say with certainty, despite fifteen different kinds of uncertainty trying to barge in.

"I just always knew," Lopez continues. "Or maybe not always, but for a long time, that I was gonna wind up having to kill somebody. So, I figured I might as well do it over here, where it's legal and it pays. Y'know?"

"I know." I think.

"But look at this, Bug," he says, holding out a hand that will not stay flat or still from the nerves.

"And you look at this, Gust," I say, holding out a hand that matches his perfectly.

Dave hitches up suddenly and weaves hard left, then right, plowing up an incline and into the thickest jungle. Lopez and I teeter and fall, flailing and rolling around in the basket before getting right again.

"I hate elephants, though," he says, appearing very much to mean it.

"I know you do," I say.

All the while, I cannot stop smiling and I cannot stop thinking one thing: Who in his right mind would rather be in school than right here?

"Focus, Manion. No daydreaming. Focus, or die."

"Yes, sir, Col. Macias." He still talks to me as if he's a teacher and I'm just a kid.

CHAPTER FIVE

My Secret Self

I have never been prouder of myself, Dad. What I am is a World-beater. I'm a World-beater like you wanted me to be, like you wouldn't believe. Like practically nobody would believe.

Because I can't really tell anybody, for one thing. Because I'm not where I'm supposed to be, and not doing what I'm supposed to be doing. Officially speaking.

Nothing new there, though, right? I was famously never where I was supposed to be and never doing what I was supposed to do. That was pretty much how I got myself sent here in the first place. Kind of a funny joke, when you think about it. Now that I'm doing these things for my country—and, I should add, doing them very well—I cannot be doing it famously at all because it is top secret.

I'm the World-beater my father prayed I would be. And he can't even know about it.

Whenever I go down to the air base at Udorn in Thailand, I take loads of photographs. I send some of them home, because Udorn is official and aboveboard, and part of my story. My untrue story. My lie of good intentions. I supposedly have a safe supply job there, liaising with the Thai fliers, the PARU, while they go off to do all the dirty dangerous stuff.

The truth is different.

I do all the dirty dangerous stuff I can get my hands on. And it's never enough, as far as I'm concerned.

Actually, I'm just a photographer. Photo-Recon is my specialty, politely going out and about, on my business of collecting as much advance visual evidence as possible of the enemy's capabilities.

I can never get all the way through that without laughing. I do take pictures, sure, but I do lots of other stuff as well. Col. Macias calls me the Shutterbug of Death, and I don't mind that one little bit.

The Army trained me, right up to my bloodshot eyeballs, in every aspect of *making* guerrilla warfare, not just taking pictures of other people doing it.

I am Bug here. Danny Manion was who I was back there.

Whenever I'm in Laos, which is most of the time, I carry no identification. I wear no standard government-issue uniform. Officially, I am not here, but in every other way I'm very much here. In fact, I am more *here* than I have ever been *anywhere* in my life.

And nobody can know, except the people who are here with me.

If I get captured, though, then I'm really, really not here. Because a soldier who is not here, and who is not here while not in uniform—then he's not *anywhere*.

He is, in short order, simply *not*. He is a not, a never was, and nobody back home can be proud or grieving or anything.

Could be scary, if one thought about it. So one does not.

Dear Daniel,

I am so proud of you. Worried, but proud. I couldn't even manage to write until the election was over. Now that it is, there is some relief in knowing that the country isn't going quite so crazy that we would elect someone like that maniac Goldwater. Forty-four states and the District of Columbia did the only sensible thing by voting Johnson, and I don't mind telling you that I do not think I will be visiting Arizona, Louisiana, Mississippi, Alabama,

Georgia, or South Carolina anytime soon. Those places must be states of insanity, states of confusion, states of chaos, but not states of the great union you are fighting for right now.

Or better, not fighting for, but photographing for. I like that, son. I like it very much. You just hold on to that supply job in Udorn, whatever it takes, and keep sending me pictures. Thailand looks like a fantastic place, and I hardly ever hear anybody on the news talk about wanting to bomb Thailand.

Goldwater probably would have thought about it, though.

Do you know what his slogan was? "In your heart you know he's right."

Hogwash. In my heart I know he's a maniac.

I wish Johnson would make me feel better, though. He has so much power now in just his hands. That Gulf of Tonkin business made me very nervous. Still does. He can do whatever he wants now, with all the power Congress gave him. What happens if North Vietnam makes him very angry?

It made me extra glad that you're in Thailand, though.

The boys say hi. They also say they cannot wait to go over there and fight with you.

I don't believe they were referring to assaulting you personally, but one never knows with those guys—with you guys—right?

Either way, don't get in any fights, Dan. Just don't fight. Take pictures. I like those.

Johnson said just before the election that he didn't intend to send American boys ten thousand miles away from home to do what Asian boys ought to be doing for themselves.

You are an American boy. That sounds to me as if you're free to come home.

I wish you could. I wish you didn't have to go after all. I wish you were here causing me sleepless nights, instead of over there causing me sleepless nights.

You don't write often enough.

Write. Do not fight. Write.

And send nice pictures.

Have to sign off now, son. My hand is getting weary and melancholy.

Love my boy.

Dad.

What a jerk, huh?

His stupid hand would be fine if he didn't insist on writing in that stupid calligraphy all the time. He blames the polio for making him teach himself calligraphy, which never made any sense to me. Things that make no sense to me make me so mad.

He works for a printing company, for crying out loud. He could have anything he wanted typeset for *free*. He could write me million-page letters that wouldn't cost him anything, and wouldn't have to make both of us so tired and melancholy, every single time.

Every single time, Dad.

CHAPTER SIX
Trailwatch

One month later and still nobody is bombing lovely Thailand.

Laos, on the other hand, has a different story to tell. Or to not tell.

Operation Barrel Roll has begun, and with it the first Air Force bombing raids on the Ho Chi Minh Trail beyond the western border of Vietnam. In the early days the bombers do all of their work in the northern part of Laos, so we don't see much, but the thunder rolls down to us loud and clear.

We had been informed that this operation was coming, and it has been of great interest to all of us here because these raids have the power to alter our day-to-day operations profoundly. Because they are bombing the very same Ho Chi Minh Trail that we and a lot of other trailwatch teams have been spending most of our time on.

In fact, if those Air Force boys do their business well enough, we could be out of a job down here.

That's the whole point, anyway, and a very desirable outcome. The sooner the trail is eliminated as a killer supply line—and make no mistake, this trail is killing our guys in bigger and bigger numbers, from North Vietnam to South Vietnam—the sooner we win this thing altogether. So no matter who gets the job done, there will be a lot of joy to go around.

But, I have to confess, I feel a little possessive. This is *my* Ho Chi Minh Trail.

"You mean, *our* Ho Chi Minh Trail," Lopez says, rolling my way to bump me with his shoulder. This, in turn, rolls me into Garvine, who shoves me back toward Lopez.

The two of them are flanking me as we lie under brush at a big bend in the trail. They have their M16s set up on tripods, while I am arranged roughly the same with my camera and telephoto lens. The difference is, I get to shoot at will, while they're under strict orders to do no such thing without Col. Macias's direct consent.

I've gotten some good bird pictures, and one of a snake the size of a javelin squiggling confidently right down the middle of the trail. The Meo guys in the team were dying to kill it so they could eat it. They even made hungry-hungry noises that sounded kind of demented under the circumstances. The boss refused to let them shoot anyway, fortunately.

This is our third straight day watching this exact spot, without so much as a breeze to stir the trees. It feels stale, in every way, except for the polite-but-insistent rain that's been washing over us all day like a fog. It could just as easily be coming up from the ground beneath us as from the sky above. More likely it's been stored in the canopy from last week's rain and is just now coming out to play.

We haven't heard any bombing for a week, and we are all thinking the same thing—that the trail is out of business and maybe so are we.

"Guess we'll be back in uniform," Garvine says.

"No," I protest. "That can't happen."

"Relax, Bug," Lopez says. "There are loads of Special Forces in Vietnam already, and more coming all the time. There's gonna be plenty for you to do, no matter what happens here."

But it will not be like here. Nothing is like here.

Working in Laos is called "Over the Fence," and for good reason. We're beyond most of the world's reach here, and most of the world's knowledge. We are the secrets in this place, and this is where my own personal secret self lives. Here is where I became Bug, the Shutterbug of Death. Here is where I thrive, where I fit, where we practically make the rules as we go, and we're great at it.

I like being completely off anybody's radar. I like being the watcher, and not the watched, for a change.

"Request denied," I say calmly, spying through my telephoto the brilliant green shoot of a new tree rising up out of the rotting trunk of an old fallen one. I snap its picture.

"Yeah, well, you might not be exactly regular Army, Bug," Garvine says, and I can feel him looking at me, rather than over the sight of his weapon, "but you still can't answer *denied* when they *request*."

I pause long enough to take four or five more pictures of nothing much, just to register my displeasure with the discussion.

"We'll just have to see about—"

Suddenly the jungle surges to something like life. It's not a great deal of noise, but there's enough hum and grumble to stir a half-dozen birds into crisscrossing flight between the trees and away. And enough to get the entire eight-man team to lock simultaneously on to that bend in the trail thirty yards down.

First to appear is a truck. It's barely a military machine, more like a khaki-colored pickup truck. There are unmistakable black-clad fighters from the North draped all over and inside the vehicle, followed by another just like it.

My camera is clicking away while the M16s and M79 grenade launchers remain poised but silent.

"Hold fire," Macias hisses down the line.

Next to me, Lopez and Garvine both growl like chained dogs.

This is recon. Sometimes it feels like a kind of kid-in-a-candy-store torture. Lots to see, but we're not allowed a single bite. This is all we get to do on reconnaissance missions. We are to gather intelligence, bring it back to the big powwow with all the other teams. And then we know.

And then, we act.

Col. Macias climbs over Garvine and wedges into the space between us. As I focus the camera on what is materializing on the trail, he whispers at me, all breath, no voice.

"Ghosts," he says.

I take my eye off the viewfinder to turn my head his way and he stops me, short and painfully, with a hard lancing index finger to my cheek. I return to finding the view.

"Keep looking, Dan. And keep shooting. Those are ghosts you are photographing. Not every day a guy gets to take pictures of ghosts, but that's what you're doing. A parade of ghosts, marching helpfully past your camera on their way to oblivion. First you shoot 'em, then eventually we all shoot 'em."

I shoot 'em. I aim and I shoot, while Col. Macias is giving me the shivers at the same time.

Right now, I don't even mind. My weapons are strapped to my sides, and my shutter bugs away.

Col. Macias rolls over Garvine to get back with the rest of the team, the Meo tribesmen who we rely on heavily for both local knowledge and tenacity, but who the boss refuses to completely trust enough to leave them alone for long.

Bombing alone is never gonna knock the Ho Chi Minh Trail warriors out of the game. That's why we remain open for business. These ghosts still skulking along the trail are all the evidence we need.

The trucks are followed by dozens more fighters on foot and bicycle. Then dozens more pulling rickshaws loaded down with guns and ammo, most likely.

The road is looking sloppy already, and I have to admire the perseverance of these guys slogging through that stuff all the time. Admire them, but don't pity them. They are ghosts, or soon will be, and they deserve—

"Well, look at that," Garvine says, pointing to a stooped gray shape as it lumbers peacefully around the bend. Looks like the Vietcong have some elephants of their own. "That is a very good idea. That thing can haul supplies for a whole battalion, and the mud don't bother him one bit."

"Boy, I'm gonna shoot that," Lopez hisses.

All I can do is stare, as the big beauty stays in line like he's just one more vehicle of war, only gorgeous.

"No shooting, Gust," I say, like I own the whole joint.

"Maybe not today . . ." he says.

And I don't think he's messing with me.

"Maybe not any day," I say.

"Who's gonna stop me, Bug? You?"

I squeeze off one after another after *another* frame of the beauteous beast. It's like I'm a fashion photographer and he's Sophia Loren.

"Gust, if I catch you harming one straw on his great patchy head, I'll slap you all over Southeast Asia."

He buries a snort of a laugh in the crook of his arm.

"You are very, very weird, Bug," Garvine suggests.

"I don't care," I say.

Even if I didn't care, I could easily understand why they might think I was weird. Killing is part of the deal. It's a very big part, as a matter of fact, and has been all along. Nobody winds up in special ops thinking that they will never have to kill.

But mostly that means killing *people*. Human people. Human people who in most cases are available for killing because they are part of some operation not unlike the one I'm part of, and so they understand the deal, too. And—and this is the real thing of the thing, I think— they are human people who are ready, willing, and able to kill me before I can kill them. Not only willing to be killing, but probably excited to do it. That's what we were told over and over again in training, and that is central to all the decision-making we do.

Elephants are different, though. You can tell with one look into their big smart faces that they are different. Too animal to be human, of course, but too human to be animal. And too innocent to be guilty. As far as I can tell, you have to be some kind of animal not to see that.

Apparently, some of my best friends are animals.

"When I get mine," my friend Garvine says from his bunk as we listen to the hard rain pound the roof of our hooch, "first thing I'm gonna do is cut off one of them big ears and make it into a kind of safari rain hat. I have never seen anything like the kind of rain they get around here, and no matter how bad it gets it doesn't seem to bother them elephants not one little bit. They don't even blink at it. I want some of that."

"Cool," Lopez says, talking to Garvine but staring over at me. "Since he's most likely gonna have two ears, you can make me a hat from the other. Fold 'em and stitch 'em up just like a couple of rawhide baseball gloves, right?"

"Right," Garvine says. "Exactly. Gonna be real nice, too, the way I do 'em. Last forever, protect you from any and all elements. People will kill to get their hands on my designer headgear. I just might stay here and go into business when my enlistment is up."

"That sounds like a great idea, man," Lopez says. "Bug, doesn't that sound like a great idea?"

He knows exactly what kind of an idea that *doesn't* sound like to me.

"One of the elements you get protected from better be the force of my boots, because if I ever see either one of you guys wearing any such thing, I'm gonna kick your head in."

My roommates could not possibly find this funnier than they are finding it right now, and the sound of their laughter is more oppressive than the relentless rain.

Macias is right about the ghosts.

As Operation Barrel Roll rolls southward, it rolls into Operation Steel Tiger, and we roll with it. We're camped out almost daily in one crook or another of the seemingly endless and magical Ho Chi Minh Trail. We observe such a steady flow, and such a varied array, of manpower-and-supply convoys that it could pass for one great big military parade like they have in Moscow. It's almost as if they want us to see what they're doing, or at any rate that they don't care whether we see them or not, because they don't believe we can do anything about it.

They're wrong about that last part anyway. We gather so much statistical, logistical, photographic intelligence about what's going down that trail that our boys farther down the road have plenty of time to plan welcome parties for when the *ghosts* in my photos reappear on the Vietnamese side of the border.

Because that's the only side of the border we're supposed to be working.

But, of course, it's the only side the North Vietnamese are supposed to be working, too.

Sometimes we just can't wait for them to arrive at the playing field, so we bring the game to them.

"That is correct," Col. Macias says, cool but urgent, into the heavy radio carried on the back of his Meo radioman. "An entire company of NVA regulars, fully loaded down with large-caliber truck-mounted Soviet antiaircraft artillery."

The convoy is making an unusually loud racket as it trundles past with all that firepower. The colonel could be talking a lot louder and still not be heard. The radio crackles with the same urgency Macias had in his own voice. Then he is on again, reading out our coordinates as he calls in an air strike on the trail for the first time on any of our patrols. This is serious business. I shoot madly with my camera as all the guys around me start setting up for action. Rifles and machine guns are shifted for mortars and rocket-propelled grenades. Our first objective is to obliterate those deadly AA guns. It's clear that, unlike what has come before, letting this parade pass unmolested is not going to be acceptable.

With a combination of hand gestures and short sharp grunts, Macias has us coordinated, fanned out into a semicircle on our ridge maybe two hundred meters above the trail. Each of us is settled into a notch or crevice, so that we are distributed on an unsteady line like the pattern on a heart monitor. I am still shooting photos reflexively when Col. Macias smacks the long lens down into the dirt and jams an M79 grenade launcher into my hands.

"I've been waiting for this," Lopez says with true excitement in his voice.

I swear I can smell it, that excitement, that frothy feeling that we're all getting at once. It's a kind of body odor, but one not quite like anything else I have ever smelled. It contains strains of sweat and sour, like somebody's just puked and wet his pants, but also better stuff like boiling potatoes and bacon and motor oil.

"Me too," I say, even though I wasn't aware until this second that I had in fact been waiting for this.

Garvine starts to say something, but only gets as far as, "Watch—" before the colonel gives the word to open fire.

And suddenly the world is just that, one big burning open fire.

My M79 barks like the devil's dog as I fire straight down at the lead vehicle towing the big gun. The right side of my head crackles with the impact but all that matters is the impact I witness below. The grenade slams straight into the driver, catching him at the shoulder and exploding before the impact can even blast him off the wheel. The engine compartment erupts in flame as the driver's head pops straight up into the air before coming back down into the barbecue.

The convoy is stopped dead, and as I reload I hear walls of heavy fire on either side of me. I look up in time to see another grenade take out the antiaircraft gun behind the truck I just whacked. Several more shells pound the ground and the trees all around the convoy, and we frantically go about reloading before any of these guys can get away.

Except, they don't appear to be going anywhere.

Zzzzzziiipp—boom! A missile with my name on it screams at me all the way up the slope, skewing upward like a wild pitch just before nailing me. I can feel the back draft as it screams into a tree about thirty feet above my head.

"Look out!" Col. Macias says, tackling me, thumping his shoulder into my left side hard enough that I slam into Lopez, who shoots off a mortar round about ninety degrees to the right of target. As the three of us tumble nearly off the ledge and down the steep embankment, the sound of close thunder right behind us matches all the firepower we have mustered so far. I glance back in time to see the rocket-like banyan tree tobogganing top-first toward the trail at break-a-whole-bunch-of-necks speed, snapping branches off all the way.

We scramble back into position as the banyan hurtles into the trail, making as much thunder and doing as much damage as we have managed so far. For several long seconds things go quiet. We remain poised for any movement, but there's nothing.

Could it be possible that that old tree did our job for us, just like that? And since the North Vietnamese were the ones who blasted the tree down in the first place, have we actually done anything at all?

Our answers come fast and loud, and those answers are *no* and *no*.

A barrage of small- and medium- caliber gunfire washes up toward us from the trail. Every living fighter down there seems to be taking cover in the great old tree that just tried to obliterate them. I take up my M16 and start returning fire into that big nest of dangerous squirrels. And all this time I'm thinking something that I've thought again and again since this whole thing started: The Vietcong has got to be the most determined and resourceful fighting force in history. There seems to be nothing you can throw at them that they don't catch and then somehow turn around in their favor.

Now that we can't see them, it almost feels like there are more Vietcong soldiers than when we could. We pour everything we have down into that tree, and into the several vehicles still visible on the road behind it. We are spraying every gulp of air with rifle and machine gun fire, launching mortar rounds and grenades as if we're pulling them straight off an endless assembly line— which we know surely is not the case and surely cannot go on.

But what choice do we have?

They are getting the dirty job done on us. The perches we nestled into so securely just a short time ago now feel totally exposed and pathetic. Bullets are whistling just over our heads and thumping into the earth below us. I hear a sharp "*Ufff,*" followed by a groany growl from Garvine, and I know he's been hit. He keeps firing, though.

The big banyan has caught fire in a couple of places, but the firefight doesn't alter at all.

There is a huge flash, then a *schwooop* as a rocket

scorches above us and thuds into the far end of our line. There are screams as the explosion knocks two of our Meo guys into the air and then sends them crash-banging down the hill straight into the enemy position as bloody mangled heaps. I watch and hope that the poor guys are as dead as they look, because every bump of the way down they are taking round after round of enemy fire.

The next new sound we hear is mechanical. I get briefly excited that it's the air strike the colonel called in at least two lifetimes ago.

It isn't. It is, in fact, practically the opposite.

At least another full enemy artillery company, possibly two, rounds the bend to catch up with the others. They're already in full-fire mode when we make visual contact, and this could not have been any better orchestrated for them if it had been a planned ambush.

We're firing all over the place now, into the tree that keeps firing back, over to the new arrivals who look fresh and act even fresher, as if they could do this all day.

For once, our discipline isn't doing us a lick of good. We always had that going for us, that and complete confidence, and that was what made us special. Now what?

"It never occurred to me . . ." Lopez says while quickly reloading and opening fire again.

He doesn't finish what he was going to say. The pressure of the odds, the concentration, the accumulating fear, kills the ability to talk anymore.

But he doesn't need to finish.

That we could lose. It never occurred to him that we could lose. I know that because it never occurred to me, either.

Until right now.

"Henry!" Col. Macias shouts down the line to his trusty radioman, who is caught up in returning whatever fire he can. Between the M79 grenade launcher on his arm and the monstrous radio pack on his back, Henry is carrying a lot more than his own weight in gear.

And his name isn't even Henry. Macias just gave all the Meo guys English names off the top of his head, and stuck with those.

"Henry!" the colonel yells for the second time. He never, ever has to yell anything twice, so we know we are already deep into uncharted territory.

He didn't even need the second shout, since dogged Henry is there, elbows-and-kneesing to within a foot of the boss. Macias grabs the radio while Henry collapses next to him like a tortoise caught crossing the highway.

"We need an extraction! We need an extraction right away!" the boss barks. There's a lot of frantic crackling in response. "Yes, I know they're almost here. But that's the air strike. We need an air*lift*, pronto. These guys are loaded for bear, and there are more arriving every second. If we don't get a lift, we don't have a chance."

There's much more frantic crackling, then an exchange of coordinates and instructions, before Col. Macias slams the radio receiver heavily into poor Henry's tortoise-shell and begins snapping off orders. "Let's go, men," he says, gesturing up the steep hill amidst the heavy canopy behind us. "The landing zone for the pickup is a quarter mile that way."

As we scramble and claw our way up, following our leader, every enemy warrior on the trail tries to blast us off the face of the earth. Missiles of one kind or another thump into the earth all around us, shaking the ground and causing all the ancient trees to tremble like they are going to give up any second. At the same time, the even scarier thunder of the Huey gunships come thwack-thwacking over our heads. They are swooping down in the opposite direction to bear down on the enemy and hopefully get them off of our tails, while we still *have* tails.

All the time we are climbing and crawling and hacking our way through the world's craziest vertical jungle toward the pickup point, the battle that we started rages on in a way my dad would call "screaming bloody murder." It sounds like the mighty US gunships are getting it as good as they are giving. The North Vietnamese have even managed to scramble some of those anti-aircraft guns into action, because we hear the unmistakable pop and screech of their shells cutting through the air. And about that time we hear the gradual withdrawal of the gunship attack.

They, like us, are not supposed to be here. If one of those choppers goes down, then that crew has disappeared into never-never-*never* land. America will disclaim any knowledge of the event, the operation, the people . . .

I cannot imagine. If I went down in such an operation and my dad could never even be told about it?

"Where are you?" Col. Macias says into Henry's loyal back as we all huddle around like a mama bear and her cubs. Garvine is groaning as Cabot, our Meo medic, packs his shoulder wound with antiseptic and bandages it.

The bullet went right through his shoulder and out the other side, which is good. He's lucky to get away with only a flesh wound, and we as a team are lucky to get away without any other major injuries.

Except for the two who were killed, that is.

"Pop smoke," comes the response, which we can all hear clearly because we're huddled so closely.

Lodge, our other remaining Meo teammate, hears the call and leaps right to it, as he's the man with the smoke flares.

"Popping smoke," he says as he loads and shoots into the sky through the narrow clearing of trees. "Popping smoke, blue," he says, just as we all see the pretty blue explosion in the sky.

"No!" Col. Macias snaps, reaching out and smacking Lodge's pith helmet down over his eyes. "No, no . . ."

The beautiful blue arc of our smoke signal is almost instantly joined in the sky by another, maybe a half mile away. And then by another in the opposite direction. Then, seconds later, by the sound of a heavy mortar round being fired from down the hill where we came from. Within seconds, the mortar shell passes overhead and then explodes in the thick jungle beyond us.

"Charlie monitors everything we say on these frequencies!" Macias snarls. "You don't call the color! You never call the color!"

The radio crackles back to life, our first incoming call that we had not initiated first. "Pop smoke. Pop smoke once more. Do not, repeat, do *not* call color."

Col. Macias reaches over toward Lodge—who right now I am both furious and sympathetic with—and does three things. He smacks the visor of his pith helmet again. He pulls another smoke canister out of his pack and sticks it in his hands. Then he smacks the pith helmet again.

Lodge looks to me like he might want to cry, as he solemnly works the canister into his launcher. He then aims for the sky, and for hope, and for better days, and blasts a red rocket up, up, and away into the atmosphere.

"Seeing red, over. Seeing red and coming in . . ." comes the most welcome voice on the radio.

"Affirmative," Macias responds. "And seeing the bird now . . ." he adds as we get up and run like mad toward the awesome green bird coming in to land and extract us from Death's big fat mouth.

I had gained a deep appreciation for the chopper pilots of this war a long time ago, but moments like this just boost my respect for them even more. It is just getting dark as the helicopter appears, flying furiously at tree-top level, the sound of hacking and smashing branches almost as loud as the engines and rotors themselves. The clearing they have chosen for our pickup zone is barely wider in circumference than the width of the bird's big blades.

Despite the ruckus that's still not finished at the bottom of the trail, somebody, or a few somebodies down there, have the spare time to turn their attention to our rescuers up here. An antiaircraft round whistles through the air, passing over the top of the chopper as it drops roughly through the opening in the canopy and bumps a hard landing on its skids right in front of us.

"Come on, come on, come on," the copilot bellows out the side door of the chopper as the pilot feathers the skids inches above the ground.

"Go on, go on, go on," Col. Macias hollers, giving each one of us a shove in the back like a football coach pushing players into the game.

In reality, we're being pushed *out* of the game. This is most apparent after Lopez, then me, then Henry, Cabot, and Lodge all have flopped into the chopper and are rolling around the floor. We look back to see Col. Macias running as fast as I ever did on my fastest day—but with the added handicap of a semiconscious Garvine on his arm—and making it look like some kind of ghoulish, bloody, three-legged race.

Macias throws Garvine up onto the deck like a big fish and then dives on himself, as out of somewhere, the trees start spraying our helicopter with rifle and machine gun fire.

We are all flattened to the deck as the copilot jumps into his seat, the pilot pulls up on the stick, and we roar out of there to the ping-ping music of bullets bouncing off of every part of the Huey. Except for the parts that the bullets shoot clean through.

Which are many. Hueys don't have a lot of armor because armor is heavy. As I feel us jump up into the sky, I agree that I'd rather be lightly dressed and up here than fully plated and still stuck on the ground.

CHAPTER SEVEN

Dang Da Nang

"**Y**ou sure dodged a bullet there . . . almost," I say from the side of Garvine's bed. We're in the hospital on the air base at Da Nang, which feels like practically the center of everything going on in this part of the world. This is the base from which the Barrel Roll and Steel Tiger bombers take off when they come over to our neighborhood to bomb the Ho Chi Minh Trail. It's also where very recently the first official American ground troops of the war hit the ground.

"Does it hurt bad?" I ask.

"Nah, nothing. Just a flesh wound."

"You're lucky you're so fleshy," I say, even though he's only got a little more meat on him than most of us.

"And you're just lucky I'm sedated. Read me the letter, Bug."

Garvine loves my dad, despite never having met him. I have, selectively, shown him some of my father's letters to me. I don't share the overly sentimental stuff, of course. The stuff that makes me angry or melancholy. That leaves out a lot of the letters, in the end. But with Garvine being laid up in the hospital, and what with him having passed up a chance to be rotated out of here in order to stick with us guys . . . well, I'd have to be some kind of rat to deny him anything right now.

He loves these letters, especially since nobody ever sends him any of his own, as far as I can tell. He loves the wording, the spirit, the heart, and the calligraphy.

As a special treat, as well as a supreme act of foolishness, I bring the letter to Garvine's bedside sight unseen. I make a big play of breaking the seal on the envelope right in front of my wounded warrior comrade. He whoops and claps, hurts his shoulder in the effort, and we both laugh.

Here goes.

Dear Son,

I do not like it. This thing that they're not calling a war, but which is looking very much like a war, is getting to the point of really worrying me. The marines have landed. Up until this point in my life that statement has always instilled hope, confidence, and optimism in the hearts of all Americans. Right now, as I hear the report on the radio, it does none of those things for me. It has me feeling sick, in fact.

I don't suppose it was news to you when three thousand, five hundred marines arrived at Da Nang. It might be no big deal to the thousands of "advisers" like yourself already stationed over there, but I can tell you, Danny, it is a very big deal to people here.

If you did know beforehand that the Marines were coming, what else did you know? What else do you know, that you cannot tell me?

I do not like it, Daniel. I'm sorry to repeat myself, sorry to add anything to your burden, if that's what I am doing. But I do not like this uneasy feeling, do not like not knowing.

It's official now. It is a war, whether the government chooses to call it that or not.

You should figure out a way to get out of there before this business gets totally out of hand. You were always adept at getting out of things, so this would appear to be a good time to put that skill to good use.

I have to sign off now. But since I've gone on about what I do not like, it's only fair that I should say what I do like before

I end. The photos you sent last time were so wonderful they almost made me happy.

You know why I cannot quite manage to be happy just now. But your pictures are miraculous. The one of the elephant was the most beautiful image I can recall ever seeing. I think you may have found your gift there, my son. That would be one positive thing to come out of this situation.

Having found that gift, be sure to bring it home.

Love,
Dad

"Ah, come *on*, Bug," Garvine says, laughing nervously at me. "You're not getting weepy on me here, are ya? Man, I got *shot* and I took it better than that."

He takes a weak swipe at grabbing the letter off of me, but I pull it away with one hand. With the other I wipe some sweat, and only sweat, out of my eyes.

"Y'know, Garvine, for a guy in a hospital bed, you sound an awful lot like someone who wants to be punched in the head."

"Ha. Sure, go on and punch me. I bet you'll still be cryin' more than I—"

Bam.

"What is wrong with you, Bug? I mean, really, is there something out of whack in your brain or something?" Garvine asks as he furiously rubs the spot above his temple where I rapped him. Gently. With no more than three of my knuckles.

"Shush," I say. Quickly and silently, I reread the letter to myself.

"Hey," Lopez says, slapping my back as he steps up to Garvine's bedside. "How's it going?"

"He punched me in the head," Garvine says.

"He did what?"

"Shush," I say, rereading the part where my father worries about what I know and cannot or will not tell him.

"Why would you punch a guy in a hospital bed, Bug? That's sick."

"Shush."

"It's because I made fun of him a little bit for crying over his dad's letter."

"Why would you make fun of a guy for crying over his dad's letter? That's sick."

"I did *not* cry," I growl, staggering my way once more to the end of the letter.

"Sure you did," Lopez says, and they're both laughing at this point. "You're cryin' right now, for cryin' out loud."

Now I'm really furious. I look up from the letter, crush it in my fist, and am about to give Lopez his own well-earned smack . . .

When it becomes obvious that the only real option is to laugh along with them. And to wipe away more sweat from my eyes.

"Hey, don't do that," Lopez says, prying the letter out of my hand and smoothing it out against his thigh. "These things are art."

I sit on the bed next to Garvine and place my hand on the punch site.

"Sorry, man," I say. "Force of habit."

He removes my hand like it's radioactive. "Yeah, well, save those habits for the bad guys."

"Ha," Lopez laughs, reading the letter now. "'. . . always adept at getting out of things.' Boy, do I love hearing from your father."

"You are *not* hearing from my father," I say, snatching my letter back. "*I* am hearing from my father. You're just butting in."

Garvine reaches out his hand and I pass him the letter.

"Hey, what's so special about him?" Lopez says.

"Him got himself shot. Go get yourself shot and I'll let you read my mail."

"Sounds fair," Lopez says. "I'll try to get myself shot, then."

"Don't get yourself shot, Lopez," Col. Macias says as he strides up to the other side of Garvine's bed.

"No, sir," Lopez says.

"How are you, son?" Macias says. He stands rigidly over Garvine, with his hands on his hips and a fatherly smile on his face.

"Feeling good, Colonel, thank you. I could probably get up and out of here any time now."

"That's good, because any time is now."

Demonstrating once more the level of toughness and/or stupidity I didn't know he had before, Garvine starts climbing out of bed. Col. Macias steps up and places two flat palms on the boy's chest, gently easing him back onto the bed.

"Whoa there, big fella," Macias says. Talking to him like he's a horse might be the smartest way to communicate with ol' Garvine, I think. "By now, I mean it could be any time now . . . not right now."

Garvine swings his big horsey head in my direction.

"I think he means soon," I say. "But you'll get some kind of advance notice. Isn't that right, Colonel?"

"Right. We're going to be reinserted into our area of operation by the same fly guys who brought us here. Possibly tomorrow, but more likely the day after. By then we should all be well rested and ready for action. Even you, Garvine, right?" He slaps our wounded comrade on the leg.

"Honestly, sir," he responds, "I'm ready now."

"Well, our ride is not, so you keep resting until I tell you to get up. Understood?"

"Yes, sir."

"We going right back to the trail, Colonel?" Lopez asks.

"Not only are we going right back to the trail," Col. Macias responds, "we're going right back to the very same point on the trail we just came out of."

Lopez, Garvine, and I all let out low groans at the same time.

"Why do we need to go back there, sir?" I ask. "I thought we did our job."

"We did," Macias says. "But, as is usually the way, Charlie is doing *his* job pretty well at the same time. Reports are that that very piece of real estate is being rebuilt and reclaimed, right down to the artillery pieces being pulled from those craters we so carefully blasted. Soon enough, the Vietcong will have them all right back in the game."

I cannot help but sigh, deep and long.

What are we doing? All that work, that patience, was for nothing. What are we doing with our time, after all?

What would I tell my dad, even if I could tell him anything?

"Either of you guys seen the CID Kids?" Col. Macias asks Lopez and me as we cross the compound from the hospital to the mess.

He calls them the CID Kids because the local tribespeople who work with us come from a program called the CIDG—Civilian Irregular Defense Group.

"Last I saw, they were just walking around the camp, checking it out," Lopez says. "Henry and Lodge said they did some ranger training here a couple years ago, so I guess it was kind of old times for them."

"Hnn," Macias grunts. He doesn't need to say anything more.

The colonel is no hater; I know that for a fact. I know from dealing with him back home, in school, through military training, and now combat here in the most foreign part of the whole big foreign world. He speaks Spanish, French, German, Italian, some Arabic and Chinese. I've heard him on more than one occasion work his way through conversations with indigenous peoples on either side of the Laos-Vietnam border, and on various sides of the invisible mountain-lowland borders that separate folks around here. I've seen him at it, and the thing is, he really makes the effort. He tries, and he cares.

But, at the same time, he refuses to ever completely give over his trust to the local people of Southeast Asia, no matter what team they seem to be playing for.

His reasoning is complicated enough to keep a person awake every night until we finally go home. And at the same time it's pretty simple: "I wouldn't trust *us*, if I were *them*," he says, whenever the subject comes up.

CHAPTER EIGHT

Recon to d-CON

Nothing gives you the feeling of being part of the action, while simultaneously being above it, like doing recon from one of the Army helicopters. Usually these birds run supplies and transport personnel in and out of operations, wherever and whatever those missions require.

It was almost like a holiday, the days we spent at Da Nang. We didn't have anything specific to do, but we got to dwell among the "official" operatives going about the business of war, more or less in plain sight.

But now we're in the sky, with Da Nang and all that far behind us, and a certain border just ahead of us.

"Good-bye, gentlemen," the chopper pilot calls out to us.

"What?" Lopez asks urgently, nervously. "What? Are we bailing out or something? What's wrong?"

He is looking at Col. Macias, who is sitting at the rear of the helicopter with a serene expression, bordering on a smirk.

"Hey," the copilot calls, getting Lopez's attention, along with everybody else's. He's pointing out his window, toward the ground beneath us. "That, right there, is where South Vietnam just became someplace else. Someplace Laos-y. Good-bye means you no longer exist. And neither do we, for that matter. So we hope to see you on the other side, someplace else, anyplace else. Until then, good luck!"

"Thanks," Lopez says. "And good luck to you."

"Thanks. We sure do need it, picking up and dropping off the likes of you cowboys."

We all laugh, partly because any laugh we can steal at this point is a valuable thing. There's otherwise a good deal of tension rippling through the team, not least because we don't feel like quite as much of a team as we once did. We lost two of our CIDG guys on our last operation—and we're heading right back to the spot where we lost them. Three more were taken out during previous operations, and unlike with regular Army units, there's no set system for rotating guys in and out. Therefore our team is steadily depleting. The Vietcong and the North Vietnamese Army appear to have the ability to grow back whatever they lose, the way reptiles regrow their tails. We're both jealous and furious about it—because everybody knows that the source of their replenishing numbers is the very Ho Chi Minh Trail that *we* are supposed to be cutting off, but are failing to do so.

The American assault helicopters are known as Guns, and the largely unarmed ones that deliver supplies, men, and bodies to and from hotspots are called Slicks. We've grown to love the Slick pilots who insert us into these situations and then extract us again when we get into trouble. They're among the bravest and most dedicated people I have ever met. And it is generally agreed that their jobs are among the most dangerous in this whole circus, tougher than what the gunship pilots have to do, by far.

But sometimes when they have put us on the ground and then go to lift off again, I am so envious that I want to jump up, grab the choppers by the skids, and smash them back to earth. That cannot be right.

What's wrong with me? What has happened to me?

"Oh, oh, oh," the copilot says, gesturing again, out his window to the ground below. There, the magnificent lush countryside has opened up, just a little, to expose a mini-convoy trudging along a short stretch of mucky road.

Two elephants pull modest trailers of something that doesn't look like militarily important anything—though it probably is.

"See that," the copilot says, like a mildly interested tour guide. "You know how you can tell those are enemy elephants and not friendly ones?"

My mind shoots instantly to my elephant friend, Dave.

"Elephants from the North have this accumulation of different-colored muds, with a certain chemical—"

Crrraaaackk!

In a flash Lopez has his rifle out and has shot the first of the two elephants. I'm in the seat behind the co-pilot, looking down through the open side of the chopper. Lopez is, was, on the other side, but has now lurched over, across from me.

Almost as quickly as his shot is off, I have brought up *my* rifle and brought it down again, right across the side of Lopez's neck. I have smashed him to the deck of the chopper and I have him pinned there, choking, while I watch through the open side of the helicopter as that poor, magnificent, noble beast comes to the realization that he's been shot. He staggers sideways, almost off the trail. He slides down the soggy slope. He tromps, clambers, thumps his way back up to where he was. Then, with blood streaming down his neck, he resumes his steady pace out of the clearing and out of our sight.

The copilot is laughing. Lopez is swinging and kicking back to his feet. I suddenly realize that there's an arm around my neck, and Col. Macias has me in a choke hold from behind my seat.

"Enough," he says.

When he relinquishes his grip and things seem to have calmed, I look around.

Henry, Cabot, and Lodge just look out the windows on the other side of the helicopter, grim and silent. Garvine, sitting in the rear next to Macias, gives me a small shrug.

I expect to see Lopez staring away from me when he scrambles back to his seat. But he's staring right at me.

"What?" I say.

"We're here to kill, Bug. Don't forget that."

"We're not here to kill innocents," I say.

"We're here to kill *everything*," he says coldly.

It feels strange when we're dropped back into the very same tiny landing zone where they picked us up last time, like some nightmare déjà vu.

"Good luck!" the copilot shouts as he practically shoves us off of his chopper before lifting off again.

It takes less time for us to get to our observation perch than it did last time, since we're going downhill rather than up. Also we aren't doing it in a hailstorm of every type of artillery flying in both directions.

In fact, the jungle is almost serene.

We work our way down, in the silence we've practiced so diligently to hone, until we find ourselves on the ridge. Our ridge. This quiet spot amidst the foliage was the flash point of so much mayhem before.

We even settle into basically our same notches, lining up our same sightings.

And sure enough, within minutes we find that the reports are accurate. All our good work is being reversed. The road is being rebuilt. Quickly, and expertly, it is being rebuilt.

And the antiaircraft artillery is being rehabilitated.

"Remarkable," Col. Macias says, with more than a little admiration.

There will be no extended photography session today. I know my assignment, which is to record what's happening and then to stop it *from* happening.

Lopez manages—as Lopez often does—to sum it all

up crisply. He even endorses a popular pesticide while he's at it.

"We're switching from recon to d-CON today, comrades," he says. "Time to kill the rats."

"Uh-oh, boys," Garvine says as he peers intently through his spyglasses.

"What?" I say. I gather my equipment to try and catch a glimpse of what he's seeing. I affix my telephoto and get a focus on the industrious work being done on the trail, and the crew doing it. "No big deal. We know what to do. We'll blast 'em away, the same way we blasted 'em away before."

"Okay," Garvine says in a voice that does not mean okay at all. "Though I don't know about you, but I've personally never blasted away a whole crew of ladies before."

"What?" Col. Macias says, and practically snaps Garvine's neck with the force of snatching the binoculars off of him.

While the colonel verifies for himself that the work crew is all female, I do my version of the same thing. I lock my viewfinder onto one after another after another of these solemn, determined women, shoveling and raking, filling and smoothing over every crater we'd so carefully blown into the terrain only a few days ago.

Quite a few of the antiaircraft guns that were central to the whole episode have already been extracted from their holes. They've been arranged right into their own little on-site nests, rather than hauled any farther up the trail. I guess the Vietcong decided after the last raid that this is as good a place as any to make a stand and welcome our superior airpower into something more like a fair fight.

I can't stop focusing on each woman, with their shovels and rakes, their overloaded bikes saddled with bags of gravel. The looks of quiet determination that grace their faces as they focus on the job before them.

"Put . . . that . . . camera . . . down . . . now," Col. Macias growls in my ear.

I have never defied this man. As far as I know, no still-living person ever has. And I'm not doing so now.

At least I don't think I am. But I can hear the autowinder whirring away for several more seconds before I feel the heavy thump of the side of Col. Macias's fist pounding my camera into the ground in front of me.

"You're acting like somebody who wants to lose his job, Manion," he says.

"No, sir, I do not want to lose my job," I say. I join the rest of the team in drawing and aiming my rifle.

At the work crew. Of women.

They're a great crew, in fact. Just as they get a stretch of gravel and turf so smooth you could lay a putting green on it, another truckload of material backs up and dumps its load. It takes off again while the ladies throw themselves furiously and without hesitation into the task of grooming another stretch of perfectly navigable road.

"All right, men," Macias says. "Here's how it goes. We wait for this stretch to finish. Then, when the truck with the next load rounds that bend, Cabot, you are to take the truck out with the grenades. That's your job and you keep at it until it's done. When you've accomplished that, you turn your attention to helping Henry wipe out those antiaircraft guns. This time we leave nothing useful behind. Turn it all to rubble. Lodge, you just keep feeding the grenades into the launchers. The rest of us—Lopez, Garvine, Manion, and myself—we focus on the personnel. Understand? We do not stop firing as long as there is one enemy standing. Is that clear?"

There are murmurs up and down the line. They could mean anything, but everyone understands that the murmurs are interpreted as acknowledgment, agreement, complicity.

"Are they even armed, though?" I say, fearing this conversation as much as anything else I've faced in battle. "They're just road crew, after all."

I feel the heat of Macias's stare as I continue to focus on the enemy below. I will not look toward him.

Garvine laughs. "You mean road*kill*."

I hear a chuckle or two from somebody or other, but it's so awkward and foreign-sounding it could just as well be coming from some freaky Laotian bird or monkey. Or nightmare birdmonkey beast that would round out this horror show perfectly.

It's just nerves. Nerves and nervous laughter, in lieu of anything else sane to do in this insane situation. Nobody is happy with this.

I can still feel the stare.

I hear the first low rumbles of the gravel truck.

Everybody is locked in place, locked on targets, locked into doing what must be done, when it must be done, because we understand why we are here.

"Ha," Garvine echoes himself, because there is not a single okay thought rippling through the brains of any of us now. It's all tension and jitters. Echoes and impulses. "Ha, roadkil—"

A *crack*. A crack, a shot. A crack shot *bangs* through the air between the women down there and the men up here. It *incinerates* every gulp of oxygen between there and here, and between here and anyplace I have ever been, and anything I have ever known.

I feel Col. Macias's attention rip away from me and I finally look toward him and then beyond him to the neat baby's eyehole in Garvine's forehead. I stare numbly, just like everybody else, for the several seconds it takes the colonel to flail and slap Garvine's face, hissing like a furious lizard. Then Col. Macias abruptly quits trying to patch that hole with his bare, strong, useless hands. He practically spikes Garvine's face into the ground before screaming, "Fire! Fire! Fire!"

And fire we do.

Fire isn't even the word. We have to convert the word *hellfire* into a verb, to properly represent what is happening now.

Every member of the team is screaming as he fires. The rocket-propelled grenade action off to my far left is almost certainly leaving me deaf in that ear. Henry is reloading the rockets of death, keeping both Cabot and Lodge armed up to the microsecond. They repay the effort by blasting that supply truck backward and sideways and up and down, until there's nothing left to indicate there was ever a truck that turned that corner, and certainly no truck crew to wish they never had.

Then our Meo grenade team comrades turn their furious power on the sequence of deadly antiaircraft nests, and the fireworks show is heavy enough to scorch our eyebrows even from this distance. Each small nest dug subtly into the trailside contains a stack of rockets. When nailed by one of our RPGs, they set off a chain of cave-canister implosions. For a moment it feels like we must have lit up half the explosives in Southeast Asia in just our modest search-and-destroy outing on this nowhere strip of Ho Chi's Highway.

But none of that really even matters. It matters, of course, in the big picture. After all, it's this very destruction we were dispatched to achieve. The very type of operation for which we are skulking around in places we're not supposed to be skulking. It is, in fact, the way we minimize the killings of American Boys by North Vietnamese Boys. By North Vietnamese *people*. By cutting off the supply of materials and . . . *personnel* . . . who travel down this very trail for that purpose.

So, that matters.

But right now, there are other matters.

We cannot stop shooting. I cannot stop shooting. At all the people I had just been shooting in a very different way. I was photographing people who were carrying out their duties, doing the stuff of war, the stuff that comes with the territory of waging war and making it possible for others to wage war. We break things in war and somebody has to fix those things before we break them again. And so on and so on.

But they were doing the *other stuff* of war. Rather than . . . trying to kill me.

Then that all changed.

I am focusing like never before. I am focusing my aim and my M16 on one and then two specific women who were a few minutes ago raking gravel in a way that was almost hypnotic, almost peaceful. I am focusing well enough that I have hit them both several times and they are on the ground and they are trying to crawl to safety in two different directions. I don't know if one direction is smart and the other one is stupid, or if it matters at all. It turns out it doesn't, because I am shooting and shooting and hitting both of them, and I can even see bits of them, of their black cotton clothing and then their blood and then whatever else is coming out of them and off of them because I am doing my job unbelievably well. I have never focused like this, not with the camera, that's for sure, and probably not with any other means of focus, either. Nobody anywhere has ever focused harder than this before. And I am not missing, ever, at all; not a single round is wasted. And I sense from everything around me that all the guys are bearing down and not wasting bullets. It is impossible to do this thing we are doing right now. Impossible to do it any better than we are doing it.

From the muzzle flashes and the shots coming our way, there's no chance there were more than maybe two shooters on their team. Very good shooters, though. And then even those muzzle flashes are dead.

I hear Col. Macias calling on the radio for an extraction.

We're scrambling up the hillside once again, just like the last time we were here. It's different, though, in that it's less frantic. There's no air assault on the position below us. There is no response fire threatening us from behind. We left no lives to threaten our lives.

Garvine needs helping to the helicopter, like he did last time. But it's more than just help this time. And this time there's no hope.

There is no such thing as silence on an airborne chopper. But, as we head back to base, pilot and copilot up front, our team seated and Garvine stretched out on the deck amidst us all, I experience a brand-new kind of silence.

Outside of recon, there has not been a minute—not one single waking moment in all the time I've been in my country's service—when nobody made a sound. It's almost as if it's an unspoken command at the center of this cyclone of *loudly* spoken commands that the boys gotta be barking. They gotta be blowing: blowing steam, blowing smoke, blowing raspberries, and above all blow*harding*. The alternative is listening to our own silences. Or worse, somebody else listening to them.

That moment has now come, and the silences that whoosh and thump around the inside of this chopper are well overpowering the howl of the engines and the *fwopp*ing of the blades.

Because of the dead guy on the floor among us. Because of what happened to him. And because of what we did in response.

You would think, or at least I would, that a bunch of guys with the same sort of backgrounds and experiences, the same exact training, the same sense of mission and willingness to leap into the most dangerous situations imaginable and execute the meanest, dirtiest deeds possible, would have a lot of the same thoughts.

Especially at a time like this. After a time like that.

But that couldn't be further from the truth.

Now, I don't know for sure what anybody else is thinking. How could I, since I have no idea what I'm thinking myself? But I have an idea. And it's an ugly idea.

When we reach camp and the fly-boys have the skids on the ground and the engine cut, it's not as if the silence gets any quieter. Col. Macias hops off the chopper and, using hand gestures alone, directs the two medics who are there to greet us. They follow his orders, as if there was anything else they were going to do with the stretcher they were carrying.

I don't move. Can't. At least not right away.

I watch as the medics carrying Garvine follow Macias down the hill from the helipad, and as Henry, Cabot, and Lodge follow behind them.

Lopez has taken several strides in the same direction and then realizes I'm not with them. He turns on his heel and comes back to where I am, still sitting in my seat.

"You waiting for some prince to come along and see if you fit the glass slipper?" he says, with a seriousness much more deadly than his words.

"Is there something wrong with you, Gust?" I ask, with a seriousness that's more than a match for his.

"Nobody's happy, Bug. Get it together, man."

"Does it not bother you, to do the things you do?"

"I don't do anything but what I'm supposed to do. What I'm trained to do. What I'm paid to do. Same as everybody else. Same as *you*."

"No. Not same as me. Not at all same as me."

"Right," he says. Then turns away, to head downhill with the rest of them. "Whatever you say, Mr. Good."

I remain frozen for several seconds more, rigid with rage. Lopez has walked to just about the same spot where he turned around last time.

Then, the freeze wears off. But the rage does nothing of the kind.

I rasp-roar like a mountain lion as I leap from the chopper and hurtle down the path toward him. I am hunting him like a lion, too, as I raise my claws just in time to catch him whirling around to confront me.

The immediate racket we make is both frightening and comical. With all the gear we both have strapped to our torsos, we sound something like a miniature car crash on impact. Rifles, pistols, knives, and canteens line up and smash up so well, we could be wearing suits of armor. Add to that my camera gear that punches into my chest hardest of all, and Lopez's dangling hand grenades, and we are lucky to avoid death on impact.

But it doesn't feel lucky. There's probably fifty feet of partially cleared, woody, scrubby trail leading from the landing pad down to the edge of the camp. And Lopez and I bang into every bump and stump along the way while we punch and kick and throttle the life out of each other.

Between the gear, the fists, the boots, the knees and elbows, the accelerated and compressed epic battle we wage before reaching bottom reminds me of fighting both of my brothers at once, if they were also highly trained and armed like ninja cowboys.

I've got position as we finally stop tumbling and reach bottom. I have Lopez pinned to the dirt with my left hand squeezing his throat. My right is cocked and coming for his nose.

Only it's *my* nose that takes the impact. This should not surprise me, as Lopez and I have fought a bunch of times, starting with our first week of training. He's lightning quick, with fists like compacted gravel. He's also fearless and tireless and, probably most important of all, doesn't seem to care one little bit about being punched in the face.

Good for him, because now I'm punching him repeatedly. We've both shaken away most of our gear, and are bare-knuckling it all around the edge of the camp. Bunches of guys have come over to watch and not do anything about it. Partly because there is a sort of *let the boys settle it* understanding around here, and partly because nothing much happens in camp for long stretches and guys need the entertainment.

There's a sort of growling murmur all around us in place of the lunkhead barking and screaming that would surround a fight in a normal place. We have to always be aware of calling too much attention to ourselves, no matter what the circumstances. Though it's never seemed more absurd than it does in this case. Every guy here wants to erupt in loud, violent appreciation of the animal behavior before them. But they're only allowed to produce the equivalent of a trumpet with a mute at the end of it, or a pistol with a silencer.

"How, Gust?" I plead while trying to bounce his thick skull off the ground. "I thought I knew you. How is it possible to do something like that?"

"Bug," he says very calmly for a person in his compromised position, "you are *all the way out of your mind.* I did, we did, what needed to be done."

Before I can say another word, he flips me with such ease and authority that I could just as well be a practice dummy.

He has me flat on my back, and I accept it. I look up into his wide, soft, confusing eyes, and try to make more sense of him, of us, of everything, than I am able to do.

"That elephant never did anything to you, Gust," I say wearily.

I can feel the beat of his heart as forcefully as I feel my own. We are breathing hard, but not yet spent. Our muscles are strained to the point of trembling, but not yet tapped out. It would appear that maximum fitness training is not without its drawbacks.

"*That* is what made you mental?" he asks, with enough obvious shock that I momentarily wonder about myself.

"Yeah," I say, thinking right now that that is the true answer. "I think so, anyway."

Our contribution to the camp's amusement seems to have worn itself out. As Lopez and I move from the kind of punches that are enjoyable to spectators and settle into the kind of internal, mental stuff that only we can see, the crowd drifts away.

"I thought you were flipping out because we failed to keep Garvine from getting killed," he says, still casually sitting on top of me as we talk. "Or because we just shot a bunch of girls to smithereens," he adds, helpfully.

What? We did those things? We did *what*?

"What?"

As I ask that, Gustavo Lopez, probably my best friend in this world, seems to finally be drained of his remaining strength. He stares down at me with a thoughtful, worried expression. Then, he falls forward and his forehead crunches the bridge of my nose with possibly the most direct hit of the day.

CHAPTER NINE

Don't Chu Lai to Me

Daniel,

You know I have been uneasy for some time. I worry about you. I worry about not knowing. I worry about what I see in the news and what seems to be an alarming turn of events in the political situation here and the aggression and geopolitical situation where you are.

Which brings me to the question of where you are.

Daniel, when I believed you were in Thailand I was relatively comforted by that thought, because everyplace else in that part of the world seemed more dangerous. Despite the fact that I had to work hard to believe you, that was still some comfort.

Do you remember Father Marcotte? From the parish? He's over there, as you may know.

And, well, Father Marcotte is sure that he saw you in a place called Chu Lai. He said he was in a moving vehicle while you were walking through the camp, otherwise he would have spoken to you. Still, he was certain it was you. Sure enough that he told his mother so.

Priests do not lie to their mothers, Daniel, as you know.

I suppose I'm wishing you were a priest right now, rather than a soldier, so that at least I could get the truth.

No, that is a lie. I wish you were neither.

See, that's the thing about lying. It gets contagious.

I love you. I miss you. I worry for you, son.

Write me something I can use?

Love,

Dad

PS The boys say they have only just now gotten all of your smell out of the house. They're just being wise guys. I know better. I can still smell you everywhere.

It can be hard to keep up with correspondence, under my current circumstances. But there are some letters that demand immediate attention. Unless you're a complete rat of a son.

Dear Dad,

"A moving vehicle." He said so himself. A MOVING vehicle. How can anybody, even a priest, have the power to tell one grunt from a thousand other grunts—when really they all look basically like me anyway—from a vehicle traveling at speed, over an almost certainly rutted and cratered road, under the stressful air base conditions in present-day Vietnam? Which, as I understand from hearing others talk, are much more stressful than anything encountered in Thailand.

While I would never question the honesty of Father Marcotte, or any other priest or their mothers, I don't think it is out of line to question the accuracy of what he thinks he might have seen.

Things are incredibly busy right now, but I promise I'll sit down soon when I have the time to write a longer letter. In the meantime, please do your best not to worry about me, because I really am fine and have every intention of remaining so.

Meantime, meantime, here is something you can use, as requested. I'm enclosing another elephant picture. I'm taking as many of those as I can. Because I discovered something about myself here, and that is how much I absolutely love elephants. I never had any idea. That has to be a good thing, right? Any guy who can love elephants has to be a quality human being, don't you think, Dad?

And I probably never would have figured this out if I didn't come to a place like this, one of the few places where you can see elephants outside a zoo or a circus.

Which, by the way, I never, ever want to see again. But I won't have to, because I'm going to bring one home with me to keep. Tell those rotten brothers of mine, if they think I created a stench before, they ain't smelled nothin' yet.

Love,

Danny

There. I think I got through it without technically telling any lies at all.

Except maybe just one. And, by the way, it involved priests, not elephants.

CHAPTER TEN

The Elephant in the Room

My film development lab is basically a carbon copy of the camp latrine that it sits uncomfortably close to. There are days—hot, downwind days—when the scents wafting up from the chemical bath used to process the film serve the extra purpose of preserving my will to live.

Today is not one of those days. It's raining steadily, and aside from the comforting red light inside and the grinding of jeeps fighting through mud outside, I'm not receiving any sensory signals—other than the ones coming up off of the photographs.

But there are plenty of those.

Elephants, of course. Birds alighting onto trees. Snakes and trucks and bicycles and goats. Big guns pulled by small people down a modest stretch of a modest miracle called the Ho Chi Minh Trail. All of these images float up to me out of the chemical soup I work with.

And all of them surprise me.

There is, of course, not a single image I haven't seen before, since I took every shot myself. But that was before. Everything is different from before, I'm learning. Every now is different from every before. Every image looks like something new when I develop it, compared to what I saw in the viewfinder. And every image looks different on a second viewing and different again on a third and a fourth.

Sometimes I blame the autowinder. Because I can press a button and keep on shooting. Things that are too fast for me to see and record and comprehend in my own head, the photo equipment can capture so easily.

Other times I decide it's a contest, a conflict between the two pieces of photo equipment that has nothing to do with me at all. The viewfinder and the autowinder. Viewfinder versus autowinder. One of them wants to see, and the other one wants to move right along as fast as possible and never linger over anything.

The autowinder only runs in one direction. Once you've viewfound and autowound, you can't go back. You can't autowind things in reverse and unview the views, no matter how badly you might want to.

Like now.

I'm developing the latest set of prints. Blooming into view, like ghosts, are the people repairing the road our guys had already destroyed once, reviving the anti-aircraft artillery we sidelined. I see them, heads down, raking and hoeing and shoveling the fresh road all smooth. Then I see the truck back its way around the bend, to deposit the road materials that those guys will work like crazy beavers to smooth out again before it returns.

Girls, that is. Not guys. Including, I see now in the images swimming before me, the shooters. Crouched behind, or beside . . . No, crouched *within* the anti-aircraft guns at either end of the work party, entwined in the gear, melded to it, are two snipers. Sniper girls.

I should have seen them the first time. Seeing things, recording what I see, noticing the details and reporting them to somebody—that is, above everything else, my assignment here. Maybe somebody else could have seen them, too, but I'm the one who *should* have seen them. I am the one who had to see them, the one who was counted on to see them.

But I didn't, until now. I didn't see them when I could have done any good, when I could have possibly saved Garvine a bullet and a box.

I can see clearly now. I can see everything and more.

I'm getting a little bombed out myself now, as I witness the indisputable reality of what I had hoped was not real. The pictures of those girls come floating up at me, out of the chemicals, out of the bath, faster than I can keep up. Somehow there's a smiling group picture, as they all look up at me over their simple farm implements. Somehow there are individual closeup portraits, like high school graduation photos, even though they all look like freshmen or sophomores to me. Somehow, I can see the shots I missed, the shots I didn't have time for, after Col. Macias ordered me to stop shooting pictures and start shooting people. I can see the shots I would have shot, after the gunfire stopped and the scrambling away started, up the hill and to the pickup zone.

They keep floating up to me, even when I'm not feeding any more film into the process. I see them all, hardworking and human, small and serious and smiling. Deadly and industrious and efficient. And focused.

Focused on me now.

The two girls I killed, the two I know for certain that I killed myself, shot and shot until they died and then shot some more until pieces flew off of them and then I shot those pieces and the pieces died. I can see them before I shot them, and I can see them as they are being shot by me. I can see them falling and crawling and sprawling. I can see them screaming, because you can see screams at least as clearly as you can hear them.

And I see them dead. Impossibly dead, remarkably clear and close. They've separated in their scramble. One had turned to the other when the first one died, with her eyes open and her tongue hanging out and touching the mud. The one behind has her hand on her comrade's shoulder, as if she'd tackled her. Her eyes are closed, but her mouth is open—along the side, where my bullets have ripped her cheek and exposed her teeth.

It should come as more of a surprise than it does that I can see this all so clearly, the images right there in the bath before me. Somehow it doesn't. But the part that does catch me off guard is that they're facing my direction, as if they were scrambling toward me instead of away.

I have no idea how long it is that I am staring down, hanging my head and contributing my own goop to the soup of the chemical bath, when I hear a knock.

"Red light's on," I say. "When the red light's on, it means keep out."

"Daniel, I don't care if the red light is on or the Blue

Moon of Kentucky," Col. Macias says gruffly. "You have ten minutes to close up your little office and get geared up. Meet me at the chopper pad."

"Yes, sir," I say, knowing that those are the only two acceptable words in response.

Eleven minutes later I'm sitting in my seat behind the Huey's copilot. I ran to my hootch, collected my camera equipment and my killing equipment, working up a healthy sweat, which mixed nicely with the rain as I sprinted to catch my ride. I didn't see any of the other guys on my way, so I figured that meant I was the last man to make it.

Which I was. But there were only the four of us: pilot, copilot, Col. Macias, and me.

"We have had a report of some unexpected movement along the trail," Macias says as I look at him with obvious confusion.

"Okay," I say. The chopper has lifted off, and we are powering over the trees, low enough that we can hear the tallest branches catching on the skids. "How come it's just us, though?"

The colonel sighs and looks out the window on his side of the bird.

"Do you remember, Manion, back when you didn't

used to question me? Do you remember those days? I remember those days, and I yearn for their return."

I pause, trying to gauge the atmosphere before speaking. But I can't. Normally I'm pretty good at that kind of thing, but I think I was ripped away from my photo processing without the proper chance to regroup.

"I don't think I can quite remember any such days, sir," I say, trying to be honest without at the same time risking my life any more than my job requires.

He opts not to overreact, which is a relief. But he doesn't lighten up much, either.

"I'm sure you'll remember, once you give it some thought. When I first met you, you were that snotty, mouthy, disrespectful punk who was always out of control and in trouble. You remember that kid, certainly?"

It would be conceding too much to answer immediately. So I give it a few extra *thwop*s of the rotor blades first. "Vaguely, I suppose, Colonel."

"Good, then we are getting somewhere. I'd be worried if you had no recollection of that troublesome young pup whatsoever. After all, you've done a great deal of work to grow out of that, and should be proud. At the same time, he is a part of your history, your path, your hash marks, and is therefore important for you to acknowledge.

Those who can't remember the past . . ." He lets that particular quote hang there.

"I don't remember the next part," I say, because apparently I have a desire to be thrown off of an airborne helicopter.

The colonel is taking an unusually serene approach to insolence at the moment, which should maybe worry me.

"Well done, Manion. You came up with an inventive way to say you know exactly what the quote is. Bravo. Now stop being inventive if you don't wish to be thrown out of an airborne helicopter."

If he knew me just a little tiny bit less deeply than he does, my whole life would be a different thing right now. The thought is both comforting and terrifying.

"Those who don't remember the past are doomed to repeat it, Col. Macias. I remember that."

"And you don't want to be doomed, do you?"

"I do not want to be doomed."

"Remember it all, Danny. Don't shy away from what you've done, or what must be done. And do not be ashamed of it."

At this, I go silent. I stop looking at him. I turn to look out my window at the very moment I become aware he's turning from his window and toward me.

"Right, so you remember. You remember both the

things you want to, and the things you don't. It makes you the man you are. You acknowledge the rascal you were in high school, and also the man you became upon entering the service. *That* man was the one who didn't question me. Remember him? That man understood the deal, that to reach the next level of your evolution, Daniel Manion, you were going to have to become the model soldier and more. The fighting machine who could do anything and everything necessary to get a difficult job done. The man who understood that orders were part of the deal. A big part. The man who understood that killing was a big part of the deal.

"You understood once, Danny, that when I point and say *kill*, that you kill. No questions, no hesitations. Your questions and hesitations could be somebody else's death. The wrong somebody. One of the good guys. Maybe me."

"We've arrived at our destination, Colonel," the pilot calls out. "We'll be dropping down in just a minute."

"Very good," Col. Macias calls back. Then he turns to me once more. "I know you know, Danny. But sometimes we need to be reminded that we know what we know. You know?"

"I . . . know," I say sluggishly. Whether it was his intention or not, I can't stop the flood of rememberings, good and bad and worse.

Of course it was his intention. Everything is always his intention.

As we pass over a clearing, down in a low hollow in the jungle, the pilot and copilot both point out my side of the chopper. Something's there. Then, Macias sees it and joins the pointing party, urging me to see.

Then, as if these things are connected, he says, "You can't be questioning your team, either. Guys doing what they have to do is hard enough without being challenged by their closest buddies."

"We'll put you guys down in the clearing higher up," the copilot says as we bank away from the scene down below. The scene I finally caught. "Then we'll take off and be back for you again in one hour. Make sure you're at the pickup zone. That should give you plenty of time to get it done."

Now I really *do* want to be thrown out of the airborne helicopter.

Except that I'd probably land on top of that great, sad, unlucky beast, still wandering in circles, still streaked with blood from Lopez's bullet.

Time to get it done.

"You couldn't really be telling me to do this, Colonel, sir."

"Why couldn't I? And also, I thought we just established that you weren't going to be questioning my decisions anymore."

I'm following Col. Macias as we hike down a tricky stretch of dense hillside jungle. I'm as close behind him as I can be without stepping on the heels of his boots, just close enough that we can communicate without risking being heard.

"With all due respect, sir, that wasn't a question. It was more of a speculation."

"Daniel, you are reminding me more and more of that wise guy kid who maybe should have been sent to jail by the judge."

"I swear, that is not my intention, sir. But . . . what does my shooting an elephant contribute to the greater . . . ?"

"*That* is a question," he says before I can even complete it. Then he raises his hand sharply to cut off any more discussion.

Several stumbling, scrambling minutes later, we emerge onto the periphery of the small clearing where the elephant has secluded himself. I have deep scratches over my hands, arms, and neck from battling through the foliage, but nothing like what the elephant is dealing with. In addition to the bullet wound in his neck, he appears to have scuffs and angry abrasions on his shoulders, his trunk, and his backside. Col. Macias has signaled for us to get down on the ground, where we're now both lining up the target the way snipers do.

I watch the elephant through the scope of my gun. He's banging himself into the trunk of one tree, then another. Then he rubs himself, too hard to be comforting, against the hard wood. He looks both crazed and innocent, trying to work out what is killing him and to fix it with even more pain.

He looks almost foolish, with his big baby head and his relatively small ears. He has two tusks of different lengths, and they look like white cigars tucked under his lip on either side of his trunk. The longer tusk, maybe a foot and a half long, also seems to be bothering him. He rams it every few seconds into a tree.

I feel my breath quicken, feel my chest pushing me up and down, off the dense turf. I think of how terrified I've been at every dentist appointment of my life. I try to imagine what an immense tooth like that must feel like when it's aching, and how madly unfair it is for him to have a bad tooth on top of everything else.

He swings his head back and forth like a crazy thing, rolling his eyes up to the sky and down to the ground, as if he is thinking, *Why me, why me?* And why shouldn't he be asking that now?

"Manion," Col. Macias says firmly, having given me all the time to get used to this he can allow.

I have never had this kind of trouble focusing on a target. I've never had any trouble whatsoever focusing on a target. The gun is steady, my hands are steady, but I blink and I blink and I blink, trying to blink this whole thing away. I'm almost convinced that after one more I'll open my eyes and find it's all over, one way or another.

"Manion," Macias says once more, with decreased patience and increased anger.

He's suffering, I finally tell myself. That poor beast is in pain. He is hurting, and now he's hurting himself.

I keep my eyes wide and dry now, as I aim true at his earhole.

Suddenly, as if he hears us or smells us or whatever magical sensory thing elephants can surely do, he turns squarely our way. He works up a head of steam, and he is charging hard—straight enough that in another five or so seconds he'll have us trampled into mulch.

The first shot rings out, slams into the front of his bulging skull, and he stops short. He stands there, confused and looking like his feelings have been hurt as much as anything else.

Then he turns ninety degrees, giving us the full side view.

"I did my part, Manion," Col. Macias says, lowering his weapon. "Now, you do yours, or I swear I will send you all the way back to that judge's courtroom."

The elephant is suffering, I say again to myself. This has to be done. There's no other way. *Do it, Dan! Do it!*

Craack. The rifle kicks. The smoke curls straight back to my nostrils.

The great big toy of a creature stumbles sideways with his two front legs, while the rear of him tries to stay planted. Then his back legs stagger into place. Then his front knees buckle and he's in praying position. His trunk rises and he attempts what was probably once a mighty trumpet.

Struggling hard, he gets back up on all four legs, only to have the back half of him give up.

Craack. I can't take it, and I shoot him again. His knees buckle again, and he's all down, legs under him like a defenseless newborn calf. He looks around for answers, does not appear to find any up in the sky, and so gives up on everything and topples all the way over.

The way he lands, he winds up with his trunk pointing

in my direction, like an accusation. Blood is pooling under him from the head and neck wounds. He tries to look right at me with his good eye, as well as the goopy hole where I've shot the other one out.

I don't even notice when Col. Macias gets up, until he kicks me medium-hard in the side to get me moving as well.

If he'd kick me much harder I might feel better.

Regardless of rank or respect or any other unreal factor of this military life, there's no way any colonel or general or commander in chief of the United States Armed Forces could force me to speak as we make our way back to the pickup zone.

Fortunately, whether it's because of uncommon perceptiveness or something else, Macias has no interest in trying.

It's starting to feel as if we truly do know every in and out of the jungle, all along the Laotian stretch of the Ho Chi Minh Trail. That's helpful as we make our way silently back to the spot where we'll rendezvous with our extraction helicopter. The only sounds I notice are the calls of birds, the minimal crunching of branches underfoot, and the screeching of all those memories I'm now ordered to live with.

Until we hear the sound of chopper blades. As we climb to within approximately fifty yards of the landing spot, Macias starts double-timing his march, crawling up the forest wall. I stick close behind, out of blind instinct and good training.

We scramble to thirty yards, then twenty, and we can see the perfectly timed descent of our fly-boy pals coming to extract us from the dangerous and decidedly unpleasant tropical killing zone we're in.

When the *thwopp*ing of the rotor blades becomes the only sound we can hear, we accelerate toward it, timing it to get there when the skids finally touch the ground.

But another sound intervenes.

Schwoooop . . . booom! A rocket sails nearly straight over our heads and slams into the side of the chopper. A half second later, a second one from the opposite side of the hill hits with a tremendous *bu-hoom!*

We lie flat on the ground to watch the helicopter with our two pals tilt sideways and hack away at heavy woodlands. The trees sound almost as sickening as breaking bones as they snap and crunch.

The chopper is mostly gold fire and black smoke as it thuds to earth and explodes on impact.

There's nothing for us to run to at the top of the hill anymore, and everything in the world to run away from.

So before we join the bonfire and the casualties list, the colonel and I angle toward a spot halfway between the two rocket nests and start barreling back down the hill, as fast as our legs will carry us.

And when our legs won't carry us, we stumble and crash and skid and somersault and jump and dive and flop our way down.

CHAPTER ELEVEN
Eye to Eye

"Can you get up?" Col. Macias asks, slapping both of my cheeks to wake me up.

"How come you get to ask questions if I can't?" I say by way of response.

He smiles broadly, close in to my face.

"That is a question, Manion. But I'm glad to see you are still with us. That was quite a tumble."

"It was quite a whole bunch of tumbles," I say.

I landed awkwardly, almost on all fours but more like an NFL lineman in his three-point stance just before the snap. Also like a lineman, I appear to have attempted to tackle a sturdy tree, which is where my shoulder is now embedded. The tree seems to be okay, though the jury is still out on me.

Macias is addressing me from the opposite side of the tree, with his shoulder leaning into it as well. Maybe I did knock the tree off its cleats, and the colonel is propping it up.

I don't believe that, but I do think it. Because it seems I got my bell rung during my personal avalanche down the hill.

"Time to take inventory," he says, reaching around the tree to get a firm grasp of my upper arm.

Slowly, I go with the momentum of his effortlessly powerful tug. I can hear all my bones and joints creaking, like the splitting old wood of a dying tree. It feels like not one square-inch patch of my surface has escaped a pulping. And nothing beneath the surface has gotten off any lighter. My elbows, shoulders, knees, and ankles feel like some sadistic torturers have been twisting them all in directions they were never intended to twist. Bruises are already whispering nastily about how they're going to torment my muscles three days from now.

But nothing appears to be broken. And there's no blood exiting my body from anyplace dire. I get to my feet and address my commanding officer in what I feel is a steady, sturdy military stance. All things considered.

"Aside from the broken nose, the blood, and whatever that slurry is pouring out of the bottom of your eye, I'd say you came away from our little mishap largely unscathed."

Unscathed. Unscathed? This is not unscathed. This is somewhat scathed. Unscathed is what Col. Macias is right now, after enduring the exact same little mishap. Aside from maybe a scuff on his forehead, he stands before me as the same cast-iron character I've known since the first time I met him.

I think now maybe even the forehead scuff is just something I'm hallucinating. It's getting watery and blurry the more I look for it.

"When we get back," he says, "we should do a little extra work on your land-and-roll technique, so you don't get so banged-up next time." He tugs gently at my belt, leading me away from where we landed, and farther away from where the wrecked helicopter never quite landed.

"My land-and-roll isn't bad. It was all those stupid trees."

"Yeah? Well I wish all my guys were as sturdy as those stupid trees. And as trustworthy, may I add."

I follow as closely as I can, but Macias is hard to keep up with at the best of times. Now my head is thumping, my body is creaking, and suddenly it's getting difficult to see. We cannot slow down, though, or Charlie will find us for sure. We have to get clear of this area.

"Are you saying I'm not trustworthy, sir?" I ask. And that thought hurts as much as everything else combined.

"Absolutely not, Danny. It's the Meo boys. I don't

know which one, but somebody in that group betrayed us to the enemy. That was an ambush. They were waiting because they were tipped off. Our little errand was unofficial, off the books, and only a very few guys knew about it. We'll know who did the ratting when we get back and see who's deserted camp. Assuming they have the sense to run before I get my claws into them, which I sincerely hope they do not."

I don't know if this distressing information has anything to do with it, but I'm rapidly running down, losing power as well as sight. We cross a shallow stream about two feet deep and maybe ten yards across, when suddenly I pitch forward into the water face-first.

Next thing I know, the colonel has me up and is carrying my soggy, sorry self to the far side of the stream and several yards beyond. He sets me down in the first available foliage, propping me in sitting position, with my back against the base of a tree that's angled like a recliner. It is not, however, relaxing.

"There's a problem," he says as he looks into my eyes with a mini pinpoint flashlight.

"Oh, is there?" I ask, trying to sound less like a wise guy and more like a numbskull.

"Ah," he says with his broad toothy smile, though I can only just about make it out. "That, my friend, is why you're here. Coolness under pressure. Or possibly just a very useful insanity."

"Either way, I'll take the compliment, Colonel. But maybe now you should tell me what the problem is."

He starts flicking the light this way and that—up and down and left and right—making me follow without moving my head. The watery blur effect is increasing, and there's an unfamiliar strain while I'm muscling my eyeballs all around.

"How do your eyes feel?"

"Up until just this minute, my eyes were the only spots on my whole body that were *not* in pain. The right one is all out of focus and syrupy, though. And there's a scratchy feeling, right around here." I point to the spot behind my right eye bone, the part that's tucked safely inside my skull, unless I look sharply to the left.

"Look sharply to your left for me."

I do my best to follow his order, and this is where things start to intensify. The scratchy feeling gets worse, like a cat is clawing away up there. And the muscles behind the eye—which I had never thought about even once in my life—feel like someone is working on them with a soldering iron.

I growl as quietly as I can, and involuntarily pull my head away from him. He's seen enough, however.

"Okay, Daniel, let's get right to it. You are not only losing blood, but your right eye has been punctured. The vitreous substance that makes up your eye structure— the egg white, basically—was stabbed from the corner by a rock or a pointed tree branch or something. That egg white, along with blood, is leaking out of you at an unsustainable rate. If something isn't done about it, your eye will be flat like a leaky tire by the morning."

Among Col. Macias's many gifts, both as a military leader and a high school teacher, is the ability to spell something out in such crisp detail that if you don't get his point, you deserve whatever happens to you.

"You know this for certain, sir?"

"I do."

I've found that stress and fear—which in this moment are both present and accounted for—have the effect of making me diversionary and inquisitive. "Just out of curiosity, Col. Macias, do you know . . . actually, *everything?*"

"I do, yes."

That should probably make me feel better. It does no such thing.

"But specific to the matter at hand, I've seen this injury before. Once, on a survival exercise, I accidentally stabbed a man in the eye."

"How do you do that accidentally, if I may ask, sir?"

"I was trying to stab him in the temple."

I am almost out of steam, and surely out of casual questions. Wooziness is taking hold.

"Colonel, what do we mean by *if something isn't done?*"

He takes a moment, and a deep breath, which is not his usual way.

"I need to stitch your eye."

"You mean, like, *around* my eye?"

"Soldier, I have to put a couple stitches *into* your eyeball, to halt the exodus of your vitreous. Otherwise you are going to lose your eye."

"The exodus of my vitreous. You make me sound a lot more complex and substantial than I deserve."

Col. Macias leans in so close I can *almost* see the details of his rugged warrior–guidance counselor face. "You deserve it."

Then he pulls back and slips off his web gear, which is a sort of complicated fishing vest for carrying the department store of survival items we're required to carry in the field. It's not nearly as loaded as usual, likely because of the unofficial, unmilitary, and frankly unnecessary nature of our outing.

He takes off his shirt, lays it out on the ground, and studies the highly detailed cloth map of the area that he's sewn in there.

"What we need," he says, snorting at whatever he's finding on the map, "is to get to that waterfall. Chopper guys have been using it as a marker for nearby LZs pretty regularly. If we can get there, we can buy ourselves a little time and breathing room, 'til somebody up there spots us. Charlie doesn't have a lot of use for that area. It's too far off the trail, and doesn't really lead to any-place strategically useful."

"Charlie isn't all sappy for beauty spots, I guess."

"Charlie doesn't have *time* for beauty spots. Not to mention that Charlie's whole world is one big beauty spot. Or at least it was, until we lit into it."

He goes totally quiet then, and focuses so intently on the map that it seems like he might disappear into it.

Suddenly, he snaps upright, pulls his shirt back on, and hitches up his web gear.

I've seen this many times. Col. Macias studies a map for a couple of minutes, inhales all its details, and then doesn't consult it again.

"Come on, Manion," he says assertively, as if he senses that I'm resistant to the plan. If I had the *capacity* to resist, I actually might. Especially after he gets to the good part. "We have three very hard miles to go, before I puncture your eye with sharp objects."

"Gee, sweep me off my feet why don'tcha, Colonel?" I say as he yanks me up into an approximation of an upright position. I immediately feel like I'm going to black out.

And so, sweeping me off my feet is what he does.

"Your only jobs now, Daniel, are to remain conscious and maintain your grip," he says. Then drapes me over his back like he's pulling on a knapsack. "I'll do the rest."

As far as divisions of labor go, you'd have to say I got a pretty good deal there. But I'm still foaming with anxiety over whether I'll be able to fulfill my part of the bargain.

I remain conscious, but without being conscious of very much of the world around me. My focus is on holding tight and holding myself up. My entire world right now extends no farther than my own head and arms, and the strong back of Col. Macias. I could be in Laos or Las Vegas, and there would be no difference. All the terrain I can sense is the shocking hardness of the colonel. He attacks the trail decisively, marching with the same steady, tenacious pace he always maintains, despite the fact that I'm clinging to his back like a baby chimp.

"Good thing we made the brilliant decision to travel so lightly today, eh, Danny?" he says, probably to keep me engaged, rather than out of any burning desire to talk. His voice doesn't give away any undue stress caused by my dead weight. I'm breathing heavier than he is. "Yes, this lack of radio, explosives, heavy weaponry, rations . . . That stuff would just be slowing us down, right?"

He's joking but he's not. This is the type of failure that'll eat at the colonel for ages. If, in fact, we have ages left to live.

We went joyriding. To shoot an elephant. Except for the animal murder element, it's exactly the kind of stunt I would have pulled in the old days. And Mr. Macias the teacher/counselor/coach would have scalped me for. I would never have thought this before—and I most likely never will again—but Macias should feel like a jerk right now.

"It's not your fault, sir," I say, pretty close to his ear. "It was one hour. It was relatively safe. We were betrayed."

"It's never safe, Daniel. Never. I should know that. I *do* know that. I dropped the ball. But it's a mistake you will never make, so that hard-learned lesson is what we can take away from this."

He steps into a hole, grunts hard, stomps back up out of it, and picks up speed as some sort of compensation. Or penance.

"You sure are one teacher who goes above and beyond to teach a lesson," I joke.

"Good teaching should never look this hard," he says.

So there will be no letup on the guilt trail today, then.

I don't know if I broke the pact about not losing consciousness. I suspect I did. But I kept the bargain on maintaining my grip, which was the really important part.

Still, it's a shock to me when I hear the invigorating *shooosh* of the waterfall just ahead.

"Dad, are we there yet?" I say, feeling pretty clever for a guy who was just piggybacked for miles over some of Earth's most unforgiving terrain.

"Does somebody have a desire to get himself chucked under a waterfall?" he responds.

"He does not. Sorry, sir."

As gently as one overtaxed man can, Col. Macias lays me down in a semi-secluded doghouse of low-lying, heavy foliage. He kneels, flashing his penlight right in my eyes. It hurts quite considerably now, and that's just the light. For the first time I start thinking seriously about the operation itself, and I feel the panic rising in me. I start hyperventilating.

"Stop that," he snaps.

"Sorry, sir," I say again, and will probably say again and again.

He sighs and pulls the light away from my eye.

"No, Daniel, I'm sorry. I realize how difficult this is. You go ahead and breathe any way you need to breathe in order to get through it. But the fact is, we have got to do this right now, before the natural light fades. And before *your* light fades. So, are you ready, kid?"

"No, sir!" I say in the most robust jolly-liar voice I can manage.

Within minutes, Col. Macias has his web gear off. He's got my web gear off. He's got my boots and socks off. He's got his map-shirt off and has laid it down, close to where our clearing meets the rushing water. He takes out his compact medical kit and, after washing and disinfecting his hands as though he is trying to remove all the skin, he places me flat on my back, on top of the shirt, by the water. My head is pointed toward the bank.

If this all goes haywire, maybe his plan is to just shove me like a felled tree into the white water.

"I like the mist," I say. "And the rushing sound." I mean it, too, very much. The effect is dreamy, soothing.

"I'm sure you do," he says. "Although I suspect the morphine likes the mist and the rushing sound at least as much as you do."

There were a couple of injections that I barely noticed a few minutes ago. I notice them now, though.

"That's fine with me," I say. "Maybe I should have some more of that before the cutting commences."

"Nope," he says, applying some thick oily gel to my throbbing eye. "But I can allow you all the antiseptic eye ointment and rushing waterfall you desire. Just say the word."

"Right," I say. "I'll let you know."

The colonel goes about his preparations in the same way I've witnessed him go about any other duties— in this life or in the previous one. Whether throwing his whole physical self into demonstrating a side-roll counter in wrestling practice, or leaning halfway across his desk at a parents' night conference to assure my dad that I had more potential than any of us really thought. Whether doing a night jump from an airplane into a fetid swamp, or diving SOG-knife-first into a spider hole to slaughter a Vietcong commando on impact, he approaches everything with the exact same cold, matter-of-fact diligence.

Just as he's doing now with my pre-op arrangements. I'm almost calmed by the combination of the waterfall—which I now understand as one more element of the man's meticulous planning—plus the sedation, plus the Macias effect.

But *almost* turns out to be not enough. Because when he pulls the protective wrapping off of the sterile medical blade, my breathing picks up again, even worse than before.

"That's fine, Dan. You breathe as hard or as soft as you want, as long as you keep breathing. But you *cannot, cannot* move. Promise me."

"I promise, sir," I squeal as I simultaneously feel myself trying to backflip into the water.

He senses it, though, and straddles my arms, pinning me under him like the wrestler-colonel that he is.

"Okay. Revised plan. Move whatever you want, Danny, or try to, except not the head. I can promise you to be extremely quick with this, but I can't promise anything else."

"Ahhhh . . . Rrrrrr!" I quietly scream as his insanely powerful legs paralyze my body. He holds my head hard to the ground. My body tries to squirm out of it, just like the insects I used to pin to the ground with my finger as a kid. He has a thumb in my good eye, which causes me to look that way automatically, exposing the extreme right corner of the damaged one. By design.

And then he cuts.

"*Wh-haaawww!*" My fingernails carve into the ground beneath me, until I feel every one of them peeling back.

"Good job, Danny! Good job. You're doing great," Col. Macias says, mopping furiously but delicately at whatever my eye is now spewing. I growl as quietly hard as I can, and continue clawing and pawing at the Laotian earth. I hear Macias scrabbling about, until I feel one more new sensation.

"*Owwwwww, ahhh, grrrr.*" All these delightful noises come out of me as I feel the needle pierce the outer wrapping of my eye. But I keep my head still. I keep my eyes where they are locked. I have no idea how I manage this.

"Good training, that's all I can say," he mutters. "Good training in the home, in school, and in the service. That's how a man like you is made, Daniel Manion."

It is the greatest compliment a guy could possibly get, and I wish I could spit the entire mouthful of it across the globe.

Where my dad could maybe enjoy it.

My dad. Oh. Oh, Dad. I'm not even here, am I?

Another puncture, another tug of the needle and thread. And another. Then a pulling sensation, a tying off, and a rapid slathering of ointment. This is quickly followed by tearing and crumpling and a swift application of an eye bandage to seal the whole thing up again. Tight and dark and padded away.

I lie still, flat on my back. Flatter on my back than I ever thought flatness of back could be achieved, in wrestling or in life.

Slowly, Col. Macias climbs off of me—rolls off of me, really—and I feel him thump to the ground alongside me. There is no motion, no sensation anywhere on all of planet Earth right now, other than the blessed water rushing furiously past our conjoined, tapped-out skulls.

CHAPTER TWELVE

The Middle of Nowhere

Dear Daniel,

Missing in Southeast Asia. That is the sum total of what our government will tell me. One would think that the most powerful nation on Earth, with the most extensive network of global intelligence services and operations, might be able to go into slightly greater detail. If they can take aerial photographs documenting every flicker of every malevolent thought Fidel Castro has in Cuba, it should not be too much to expect that level of specificity elsewhere. Such as when informing the family of a war hero that they have somehow misplaced that hero—because that is what you are, son, a misplaced hero—in a very dangerous part of the world. They should do better than to cast a net as wide as all of Southeast Asia. I trust you are quite aware *by now what a sprawling swath of the globe Southeast Asia actually is.*

The fact that you're missing is unsettling enough, Daniel. Being missing in such a vast place is the stuff of nightmares.

I suspect this letter will never make it to you, even if I knew where to send it. I don't care. I will continue writing. I will continue sending. I will continue expecting.

Love,

Dad

There is no such thing as time or place. I don't know when I'm awake or asleep. I would say that I don't know whether I'm alive or dead, except for the fact that Col. Macias leans hard into my ear every once in a while and says, "Are you still with me, kid? Stay with me, right? You will stay with me."

Sometimes I summon the strength and focus to snap back with, "Where else am I gonna go? I can't get anywhere unless you're carrying me. And even then, I'll be staying with you, right?"

That response pleases him. Even though I have no idea how many times I've trotted it out for him. Genuinely, no idea.

But mostly I just groan. I do a lot of groaning, usually until the colonel insists that I knock it off and act like an elite fighting man. I knock it off right away when he says that.

He changes my eye dressing as often as is sensible, considering our much-limited supplies and the uncertainty of how long we'll be on our own. While my eye goop has apparently stopped leaking out of me, there's very little else we can say for sure about my condition. The colonel diligently asks me about my sight during the few minutes between de-bandaging and re-bandaging, and I diligently report that it's like looking through Vaseline. Then, when he patches me up again, the same feeling returns, where I can't tell where the squishy ooze of the ointment ends and the squishy ooze of my eye begins.

It's likely that I've developed an infection. I have a furious fever most of the time, struggle to keep my good eye open in the rare moments when I even want to, and spend most of my elite fighting training in battling relentless dreams. Daydreams, nightdreams, netherdreams. None of them nice dreams.

I think if you spend enough time with your eyes closed, you'll eventually see everything you have ever done.

And it will look far worse than it did the first time.

You will shoot and kill one of Earth's truest, greatest inhabitants for no good reason. You'll see the scope of the elephant's brilliance clearly through the scope of a rifle. And you'll pull the trigger anyway.

You will join with an armed mob of men in raining overwhelming fire down on a mostly unarmed crew of working women. You'll fire away until they are dead. You'll keep firing even after they're dead, even as pieces fly off them. You'll keep firing until they stop moving, which they cannot actually do until you stop shooting them. And then you'll fire some more.

You saw them. Clearly. You see them more clearly now, when seeing anything else is hard to do.

There's a canteen dribbling water over my lips, and Col. Macias is chattering words into my ear.

"Are you capable, Daniel?" he asks. I come to the realization that he has been talking to me for some time now.

"You know I'm capable, sir. That's why I'm here. I knew what the deal was. I knew I would have to do some killing as part of my assignment. I didn't know or expect that I would be required to put bullets into the big beautiful head of an innocent elephant, or that I would be required to shred the daylights out of a bunch of girls who weren't doing anything but fixing a road. The worst thing I ever did to a girl before that was try to kiss her without being invited to. And for that I got a punch in the face. These girls never even got the chance to punch me in the face.

"I thought I was just going to kill guys here. But when I had to do all that other stuff, I did it. So, yes, I think I am capable. Sir."

There's something like silence as the colonel helps me up into a sitting position. Then I notice a sound. A very distinctive sound, unlike all the jungle chirping and water swooshing I've gotten used to over the week or ten or twelve days we've been stuck out here.

It's a plane.

"All that notwithstanding, Manion," he finally says, "I was just asking if you were capable of moving. It looks like we might be getting rescued."

"Oh," I say.

Though I'm only sitting, I already feel dizzy from the act of getting even partially upright. My patched eye is throbbing like it's trying to blast itself right out of my stupid skull. I hope it's true that we're getting rescued, because we have pretty much run out of anything that would be usable for replacing my eye dressing even one more time. It feels soaked through, and I'm sure I can smell that certain scent of infection coming down from my own eyehole. I'm waving away insects so regularly I'm starting to think they want to make a nest out of whatever's left of my right eye socket.

And the left one isn't doing so great, either. It's strained and light-sensitive and dried out from doing all the sight work. Macias is actually helping out with the shoo-fly action of debugging my head. I can't imagine how horrific I look from his angle.

Plane or no plane, we have to move.

"I'm capable, sir," I say as I gradually become more used to being up off my back.

"Excellent," he says. "I'll climb to the top of that tree there and signal that spotter plane before it leaves the area."

He sticks the canteen into my hand, along with a small chunk of the complete mystery meat that's been keeping us alive these past several days. I just think of it as *raw, salty, chewy, dead, native Laotian creature*. Then he scampers toward the tree.

"Colonel," I say before he can get far.

"Yes, Daniel," he says impatiently.

"Could we have saved Garvine's life? If we'd been on the ball that day?"

He does not hesitate.

"No. Nobody can save anybody's life. That is a power neither you nor I nor anybody else has. So don't flatter yourself, and don't burden yourself. Nobody can save a life. The closest you can come is to postpone a death."

He stares at me a few more seconds with an "Anything else?" expression.

I just take a bite of my animal cracker. He begins scaling his tree.

"We have to get to higher ground," Col. Macias says as we set off, away from the waterside that has been our home and life source. "They saw my mirror signal and signaled back. We know they're coming for us but we don't know when, where, or how exactly. So the only thing we can do is get to the highest ground possible, while staying within the vicinity of where they saw the signal."

"Yes, sir," I say as he begins once again to drape me over his back the same way he did when he got me here. I don't feel quite as damaged as I did then, but at the same time I'm somehow more woozy and wobbly. The many days of inactivity have left my muscles feeling boiled and stretched. But after a few strides of the old zombie and son routine, I think we can do better.

"Sir," I say, pulling up on his shoulders like the reins of a horse.

"No time," he answers, dragging me along several more yards.

"I can walk," I say.

He stops. "You can?"

"I can try, anyway. With a little help."

In one swift, smooth motion, Col. Macias swings me from being his backpack to being his shoulder pad. We walk like this for a time, quickly getting the three-legged race rhythm together.

"Frankly," he says, "this is a bit of a relief. I'm not feeling quite as strong as when I carried you before. I think somehow you've put on weight while we've been here on holiday. All that lying lazy by the water."

"Yeah," I say, "and the rich food you were forcing on me. What was that, anyway? I was afraid to ask before, but since I won't have to eat it anymore I guess I can know without puking. Was it snake? It was snake, I'm guessing."

He hesitates before answering, the steady clomping of our boots up the path making it more noticeable.

"It was not snake."

"Don't tell me it was some kind of rodent."

"I will not tell you it was some kind of rodent."

"Can I get a hint?"

"I suppose, sure. Let's say it would make sense to find that you'd gained weight from eating the flesh of this particular creature."

For a few seconds, I'm finding this almost fun, this guessing game, this distraction from the mess we're in and the danger ahead. For a very few seconds. Then the fun ends with a thump.

"Let go of me!" I shout, pulling away from the colonel. He tries to hang on to me, but doesn't use too much of his superior strength. He lets go, and I spin away from him, into the low green growth beside the path, onto my hands and knees.

I spend what feels like an hour down there, heaving my empty guts out, until I topple sideways and prop myself on one hip and one hand. Macias is right there beside me, clasping my shoulder.

"He saved your life, Dan. Try and see it that way."

"I *killed* him," I say. "He gave me life, I gave him death." And for the first time I can remember, and possibly the first time in my life as far as I can think, I start crying, sobbing and bawling into the ground. I punch the earth with my free hand and let myself fall face-first into the foliage. "He saved my life and I took his. That's great, Col. Macias. That is just fantastic. You should have just let me die. You had no right. No right to do—"

In his swiftest and strongest move of the day, Col. Macias grabs a fistful of shirt at the back of my neck with one hand, yanks me up toward him, and smacks me mightily across the face with the other. My mouth feels instantly puffy, but my crying ceases, as if he has ripped my tear ducts right out. My bandages are more soaked and rotten smelling than ever.

"Grow up, soldier. Grow up and *live*. There was zero chance I was going to allow you to die then, and there is zero chance I am going to allow it now."

"Yes, sir," I say as he pulls me all the way to my feet with the strength of his one arm.

"Do you hear that sound?" he says, gesturing up the hill, where the engine of some small aircraft is buzzing away on the other side.

"Yes, Colonel."

"Good, because we have to *run* into position to signal that aircraft before it flies right over us and away again." He takes out his signal mirror and points straight uphill. "I can't drag you now, Daniel, so I'm going to scramble as fast as possible to the first viable clearing. You make your way up there any way you can."

"If I can," I say, though I don't mean to say it, wish I hadn't said it.

"Are you developing a taste for slaps or something, Manion?"

"No, sir."

"You were trained for this, soldier. Now do it."

"I will," I say firmly, and he starts hightailing it up the hill. "Might even pass you before you get there!" I add, just a bit of the old spirit creeping back up.

"That's the stuff," he calls back.

That feels good.

It is, however, the only thing that feels good right now—in my head, in my stomach, in my heart.

CHAPTER THIRTEEN

Crawlin' and Bawlin'

The truth is, I crawl like a baby most of the way up the hill. It's been my big baby day, I guess, with all the crawlin' and bawlin'.

I get far enough to see when Col. Macias's mirror catches the attention of the spotter plane. It's an extremely cool O-2 Skymaster, the kind they call Mixmaster because it has front and rear propellers for hoverability, and a twin-fin tail. I see the flash of the O-2's response, followed immediately by first one and then a second jumper, parachuting toward the ground before the plane turns for home.

This is a great sight, a welcome sight, and the last real thing I see for quite some time, as my crawl up the mountain takes me another couple of hours.

When I finally reach Col. Macias, plenty has happened. The rescuers have already found him, and they're all huddling over the colonel's map-shirt. For a moment it feels as if I wasn't even expected.

Then Lopez looks up.

"Hey! Hey!" he calls, scrambling down twenty feet of ground to meet me. He picks me up off the ground and hustles me up to where the other two guys are sitting.

"Where have you been?" Col. Macias says with a slight smile. "Another ten minutes and we were going to leave without you."

"I was taking advantage of the rare opportunity to see the country right up close," I say.

Macias laughs. Lopez takes my chin in his hand and examines my face intently.

"What happened to your eye, Bug?"

"What, this?" I say, pointing at my pirate patch. "It just got a little irritated, from that fight we had. But because you're such a patty-caker it took forever to even swell up."

"Well, then, good for me," Lopez says, "because you look a lot better this way."

"Actually, I hit him," Macias says, not inaccurately. I look up in his direction again and only just notice that the man standing beside him is Henry, and he's carrying the radio on his back.

"Henry!" I say, very happy to see him still with us. Then I think on it. "Where are Cabot and Lodge?" I ask cautiously.

"Got themselves killed," Lopez says. "Not long after your chopper was shot down."

"The way I understand it," Macias says, "it was friendly fire. As they were trying to run out of the camp."

"Friendly?" I ask, looking toward Lopez. "Who was it . . . you?"

He smiles broadly at me, then points a friendly-fire finger in the direction of Radioman Henry.

I look to Henry, who gives me a shy, modest smile and then goes back to studying the map.

"Right," Macias says definitively. "Time to call this in."

Henry hands him the radio as Lopez leans close to me and says, "See that radio thing? Comes in handy, you know? Might want to think about taking one with you next time you go out on a field trip."

"Please, Gust," I say. "Not now. Go easy on me, here. I don't think I could handle it just yet. Still a little bit weak, you know?"

"Okay, weakling, you got a deal. For now. But I brought you something that I think you'll be able to handle pretty well."

He reaches into a pouch attached to his web gear and pulls out a stack of letters. Letters addressed to me, in a familiar fancy lettering.

"They've been coming every day or two lately," he says, laughing as I snatch the whole bunch out of his hand in a wink of one good eye.

Dear Son,

I am still here. Wherever you are, I am still here. I will always be here, waiting for you to come back. I never doubt for one moment that you'll do just that, and I will be waiting. Maybe you're on your way to home right now, for all I know.

I don't need to know everything, and I don't expect to know everything. Whatever you're doing, I'm certain it's important and that you are carrying out your duties with such skill and courage that I would be bursting with pride.

I am, in fact, bursting with pride, despite not knowing.

Not knowing, I have to confess, is supremely difficult.

Write soon. I'll write sooner.

Love,

Dad

Dear Daniel,

People ask about you every day. Without fail, every day. Folks at the printing plant, at the market, even teachers at the school, when I have to go down there and deal with some episode or another involving those scamp brothers of yours. Oh, they're fine. They are good boys, just in need of a bit more than most, in terms of guidance. But you'd know a thing or two about that, wouldn't you, my boy?

You know, I almost miss it. Even your rambunctious mayhem.

Who among us would ever have thought that possible, eh, my boy?

Mr. Macias isn't at the school anymore, which apparently I'm late in knowing. He reenlisted in the service. Why anyone would want to do that in this day and age, with the way things are going, is beyond me entirely. Do you know anything about this? Speaking of guidance: That was one person who did you a great deal of good. A fine man there, Mr. Macias. I hope he's all right.

You take care of yourself, Dan. I still expect to see you strolling through the front door any time now. But perhaps you should give me a bit of advance notice, so that you don't give me a stroke or anything. I don't suppose either one of us would like that very much, would we?

It would still be worth it, however, just to see you back and safe.

My good eye is going all gooey at this point, to the extent that it's getting nearly impossible to read. I keep dabbing and wiping and reading as best I can.

Why would he say something like that? About a stroke? How is he? This must be killing him, all these questions about where I am. I am going to write him a million letters as soon as I get back to camp, let him know everything is all right.

His calligraphy isn't right. That last letter looks like someone else wrote it, it's so shaky and rough. It's better than anybody else's calligraphy, of course, but not altogether up to my dad's usual standard. I hope he's all right. I hope my ratface brothers aren't making things difficult. I'll kill them. I know how, fifty-five different ways.

Dad shouldn't have to go down to the school to sort them out. Mr. Macias would have sorted them out, sorted them *right* out, if he were still there.

But he's not. He's here. Sorting *me* out.

"Daniel," Col. Macias says. Then both of his hands are on my shoulders as I begin tearing open the next letter.

I look up into his suddenly soft face.

"Those will have to wait, son."

"My dad says hello," I say. "And thanks." I'm finding myself getting weary and bleary.

"What?" the colonel says, startled.

"Don't worry," I say. "He doesn't know you're here with me. He's talking about before. Back home. School . . . and the rest. Says you're a fine man."

"Ah," he says, relaxing slightly and then looking sharply into me. "Well, your father is as fine a man as they come. I'm planning on telling him that myself when I get back. But right now, we have a rendezvous to make. The timing must be precise or it won't happen. And, if I may be blunt in the interest of brevity, you dying here, *over the fence*, means your father will never know what became of you."

If ever there was a cold splash of water to snap a soldier to attention, that was surely the water.

"Let's go," I say.

By now it must simply be reflex for him, but on the word *go*, Col. Macias seizes me in the old familiar three-legged race grip. He's got my arm slung over his shoulders and *his* arm around my back. He's already leaning into the first strides of the trip to rendezvous when we're accosted by Lopez, who jumps into our path.

"Sir," Lopez says, "two highly trained, equipped, and well-rested Special Forces operatives have been sent out into the field to retrieve two weary and wounded Special Forces brothers. Could you allow us to do that, please?"

While I'm getting more drained and disoriented by the minute, I can still recognize that as a major-league jump into the breach from my old pal Gustavo Lopez.

And even better, Col. Macias recognizes it as such. He gives Lopez a look that says, "Maybe just this once," then hands me over to Gust. Henry leads us along the assigned path, to the tiny patch of opportunity that awaits us a half mile uphill.

Because there's nothing remotely resembling a landing zone anywhere around here, and because the whole once-sleepy two-mile radius around our beloved waterfall has become increasingly hot with VC snipers, we have few options for this operation.

We hear the chopper coming very low over the hill, just above the treetops, when we gather ourselves at the tiny clearing, no bigger than a picnic table.

"Right, now, just like this," Lopez says, producing out of his web gear a canvas belt that looks like it was made for strapping heavy loads together on a moving van. With that belt, he binds me to him so tightly that we have to take turns breathing. We are belly-to-belly, and as the chopper comes loud and close but still out of view, he hugs me hard and tells me, "We got this."

A couple of feet behind me, I hear the same exchange between Henry and Macias.

"We do," says Macias, because he can never just listen and accept something. "We got this."

In less than an instant, the chopper has found us. The way it's bearing down, hovering directly above our ridiculously tiny opening in the lush Laotian canopy, it feels as much a threat as salvation. The power of the rotor rush practically flattens us to the ground. But with Gust and Henry in charge, nothing like that is happening here.

"Hold tight," Gust says, "like you never held tight before."

I do exactly that. And the next thing I know, the two of us have grabbed on to the rope ladder lowered from the helicopter. Gust practically has to drag me, but between the two of us we make it up two, three, four, five rungs, enough for the other pair to climb on behind us.

"Go, go, go, go!" Henry calls, when he and Col. Macias have secured themselves to the ladder.

The chopper pilots don't have to be told twice, much less four times. They take off, up, and away, with such thrust that we're trailing behind the helicopter like a kite tail.

When we've gotten some height above the tree line, one of the crew shouts down, "Don't climb. We'll reel you in."

In a couple of seconds I realize why he had to say that, as I feel Henry's head bumping up against my butt. Those guys were anxious enough to get aboard that they were willing to pass us by to do it.

They're anxious for good reason.

We're not more than sixty seconds out of the pickup zone when the sound kicks off.

Rattatataaatatatatatatattaaatatata!

The rifle and machine gun fire feels like it comes at us from all angles. We're a blimp above a baseball game, where the first, second, and third basemen have AK-47s, and the pitcher, catcher, shortstop, and outfielders are all aiming up with snipers' rifles.

This area *surely* has become hot since we first arrived at the waterfall. It'd be nice to think that it was all because of us.

I feel a bullet tear into my upper right thigh. Then another one burns through my left calf.

The heroic crew member who shouted at us to just hang there is now hauling us up through the hail of bullets, like the world's bravest, craziest, strongest marlin fisherman.

When he's finally hauled all us fish on board, I can barely look around me. I still hear the bullet rounds pinging across the chopper, inside and out. I sense that all four of us are laid out along the deck of the helicopter as at least two medics work us over. Then the bullet pings are decreasing, and I raise my head to look to my right, past and over my bad eye, trying to get a half-decent look at the other guys along the line.

While nothing is at all sure in this moment, I think I see the last man lying is Col. Macias. He has pops and punctures pulsing blood out of him anywhere you care to look.

I decide I *don't* care to look, which is just as well, because at that instant a medic jams a needle into my arm and all is swiftly gone to black.

CHAPTER FOURTEEN

Like Fathers

Hey Ho Danno,

In case you didn't guess, this isn't Dad. I started out trying to do his stupid cally-graphy thing, but that wouldn't have fooled you, either.

Don't know where you are, or what you're doing, but I just hope you are killing heaps of the people who need killing. Not that I have any respect for you or anything, but I bet you are. And I bet you're doing a good job of it.

Okay, though, see, Dad's not all that good. He doesn't go to work a lot of days. You know the plant and how they treat him with his polio and stuff. They are great. He's not great. He wasn't even able to keep writing, really. Not the way he wanted to, but he kept on trying. When he got too shaky, can you believe he even tried to go back to the right hand to write to you? THE BAD ONE. That's when I had it, Danny

Boy. That's when I had to take over. Took his pens right away from him and everything.

I'm not supposed to be doing this. He made me promise I would not do this. But hey, who knows better than you do about doing what you're not supposed to do? Right? Who taught ME about not doing what you're supposed to do and doing what you're not supposed to do?

But anyway, he's not doing so good. Just so you know. Just so somebody told you. Because he never would, and anyway now he can't even if he wants to.

Not that you will even know, or even get this. Not that you could even do anything about it if you did get it. But somebody should at least try and tell you. Wherever you are.

Where are you, Dan? Are you even out there? Are you even Dan? Where are you?

Well, that's that, anyway. If you do come home, I'll slap you silly.

See ya.

Edgar, your Lord and Master

I have two medical operations in Thailand, where I do officially exist. They completely undo and redo my eye, bringing it to the point of viability, if not complete functionality. There are at least two more operations to come once I return to the United States.

But whatever I wind up with, it's already a given that Col. Macias saved both my life and my eye.

Of the trailwatch team of highly trained, dedicated Special Operations operatives I started out with—overseeing movements on the Ho Chi Minh Trail—there is now only me.

Technically, they're all gone, like they never existed. While I get to head back home.

But I remember. I remember every one of them, and I carry them home with me. And in that small way, at least, no one gets left behind.

Dad,

I'm coming home.

I have much to tell you.

And I have much to bring back, as a soldier, a student, a son, and a man.

You don't have to worry about me anymore.

But tell those brothers of mine, I'm coming to keep my eye on them.

Love,

Dan

About the Author

Chris Lynch is the author of numerous acclaimed books for middle-grade and teen readers, including the Cyberia series and the National Book Award finalist *Inexcusable*. He teaches in the Lesley University creative writing MFA program, and divides his time between Massachusetts and Scotland.